Stranded on TERROR ISLAND

LEE RODDY

PUBLISHING

Colorado Springs, Colorado

STRANDED ON TERROR ISLAND
Copyright © 1997 by Lee Roddy. All rights reserved. International copyright
secured.

Library of Congress Cataloging-in-Publication Data
Roddy, Lee, 1921-
      Stranded on Terror Island / Lee Roddy.
            p. cm. —— (A Ladd family adventure ; 14)
      Summary: .
      ISBN 1-56179-349-3
      [1. Wilderness stories. 2. Adventure and adventures.——Fiction.
3. Christian life——Fiction.]
I. Title. II. Series: Roddy, Lee, 1921- Ladd family adventure ; 14.
PZ7.R6Cas   1995
[Fic]——dc20   94-41646
                                            CIP
                                          AC

Published by Focus on the Family Publishing, Colorado Springs, Colorado 80995.
Distributed in the U.S.A. and Canada by Word Books, Dallas, Texas.

The author is represented by the literary agency of Alive Communications, 1465
Kelly Johnson Blvd., Suite 320, Colorado Springs, CO 80920.

This is a work of fiction, and any resemblance between the characters in this book
and real persons is coincidental.

Editor: Larry K. Weeden
Cover Illustration: Bob Larkin
Cover Design: James Lebbad

Printed in the United States of America

97 98 99 00/10 9 8 7 6 5 4 3 2 1

to Mrs. Carol Holt,

fourth-grade teacher

at Forest Lake Christian School

in Auburn, California

CONTENTS

Acknowledgments

ACKNOWLEDGMENTS

The author wishes to express his deep appreciation for interviews and information provided by dozens of people in Alaska, especially those who contributed to the research for this book, including:

Miss Stacy Edwards and Franklin Blodgett of Eagle River; Civil Air Patrol pilot Ed Ross, observer Charley Ricci, and Captain Kevin McClure; the Rev. Doug Stude of Sitka; Ray and Petrea Arno of the Lion and Lamb Bookstore in Homer; former Alaska governor Jay S. Hammond of Port Alsworth; students of Stacy Christiansen, sixth-grade teacher; and Duranda Howatt, fourth-grade teacher (both of Anchorage's Grace Christian School); Jill Shepard, senior editor at *Alaska* Magazine; Bruce Merrell, Loussac Public Library, Alaska Collection; Marie Ward of Fairbanks; and Lorene Harrison, a real Alaskan pioneer, age 91, for her shared memories of early territorial days in Anchorage.

Chapter One

TROUBLE ON THE TRAIL

Josh Ladd stopped on the Alaskan mountain trail and turned, surprised, his dark blue eyes on his best friend. "You sound upset," he said.

"I am!" Tank Catlett shot back. He rocked slightly on his feet, his new hiking boots squeaking. "She thinks she knows everything." His pale blue eyes flashed ahead 50 yards to where Alicia Wharton and her father had paused to admire the spring flowers growing beside the rocky trail. "She talks to you all the time and ignores me, and when I try to say anything, she looks at me as if I don't know what I'm talking about."

"I don't think she talks more to me than to you."

"Well, she does!"

"If that's true, maybe she senses you don't like her."

"I don't, and that's for sure! So why doesn't she just leave us alone? You and I've been friends since we were babies, and we don't need anyone else—especially her—hanging around. But she's been butting in like a know-it-all ever since we met her in Hawaii before we moved here."

1

"She's just trying to help us learn about Alaska," Josh replied mildly. He lifted his green baseball cap and readjusted it over his wavy brown hair. "Forget it."

Tank vigorously shook his head, making his pale blond hair flip around. "I can't!" he snapped, deviating again from his usual slow manner of speaking. "And why are you always taking her side?" he added sharply.

Josh stalled before answering. He shifted his backpack, which held extra hiking boots, two lunches, fruit, dried jerky, and a first-aid kit. "I'm not taking anybody's side," he said softly, hoping to calm Tank down. "I just think she's trying to help—"

"Well, I don't!" Tank broke in angrily. "She's always talking to you and ignoring me as if I were just a pebble in her path."

"That's silly," Josh replied without thinking, and instantly he saw from Tank's reaction that it was the wrong thing to say.

"Is that so?" Tank challenged, scowling. "Well then, you run and catch up with her and her dad. Have a great ol' time! I'm going back."

Josh stared in surprise as Tank spun around and started walking rapidly down the narrow, brush-lined trail. "Wait!" Josh called. When he was ignored, Josh jogged toward his friend. "Wait up, Tank!"

"This has been going on for too long!" Tank called over his shoulder. "Now leave me alone!"

Reluctantly, Josh stopped and shook his head until the other boy vanished around a curve in the trail. It wasn't like easygoing Tank to act this way. Josh was so lost in thought that he only vaguely heard Alicia and her father coming up behind him.

"Where's he going?" Alicia asked as she drew closer.

Josh turned to face the father and daughter, unwilling to admit the truth. "Uh . . . he decided to go back to his house. He'll be all right."

"But why?" Alicia persisted.

Josh thoughtfully studied the 12-year-old girl. She wore blue jeans and a light rain jacket but no hat. Her gray eyes were wide with curiosity under her blonde, pixie-style hair.

"It's sort of personal," Josh answered evasively.

"It's the first time I've ever seen him look angry," Alicia observed.

"He's about the easiest guy in the world to get along with," Josh said firmly. "But over the years that we've been friends, we've sometimes disagreed."

"Like now?" Alicia's father asked.

Josh nodded, looking up at the medium-height man in hopes he would drop the subject. Josh liked Trent Wharton, whose steely gray eyes seemed to see everything.

A widower, bush pilot, and businessman with only one child, Mr. Wharton had been largely responsible for convincing Josh's parents to move from Hawaii to Alaska. That was after Tank's father was transferred to the forty-ninth state to manage a large chain department store in Anchorage,* Alaska's largest city.

Mr. Wharton glanced at the gray sky, then lightly touched his daughter's arm. "Come on, honey," he said. "Let's get to

---

* The definition and pronunciation of words marked by asterisks are contained in a glossary at the end of the book.

that mountain we're going to climb before those rain clouds move over us. You coming, Josh?"

"No, I think I'd better follow Tank."

"Oh, let Tank go!" Alicia urged. "It's only a half-hour walk back to the house. Besides, he's got his bear spray, so he'll be okay by himself. Come on, Josh. Dad wants to show us that mountain."

While Josh hesitated, Mr. Wharton remarked, "If Tank is unhappy, perhaps it's best to leave him alone for now."

Josh wasn't sure about that, but Alicia urged him again, and slowly, the boy agreed. "Okay," he replied, "let's go climb that mountain."

The trio moved up the trail under a threatening sky, climbing through green mountain passes. Snow still clung to the crevices and high peaks. Late June warmth caused wild lupine and columbine to bloom everywhere.

Josh periodically turned to glance back, his thoughts on Tank, while Alicia and her father described the mountain they were about to climb.

"Except for pilots flying over it, few people ever see it," Mr. Wharton said. "It's hidden in a great valley here in Chugach* State Park."

"That's not surprising," Alicia added. "Even though we're only a few miles outside Anchorage, this is like the real Alaska—real wilderness. I'm just sorry Tank isn't going to be with us."

"Me, too," Josh said softly, wondering if Tank were going to stay angry with him and how he could get Tank to befriend Alicia.

Conversation dropped off as the climbing became steeper and everyone was puffing from exertion. That was all right with Josh, because he didn't feel much like talking anymore.

At the top of a green peak, the trio stopped to rest and admire the magnificent scenery spread in a small valley below them. At the bottom of two steep hills, Josh's eyes skimmed along a silver thread of river that glistened like morning sunlight on a single strand of spider web.

"Isn't this incredible?" Alicia asked breathlessly, easing the red pack off her back and flexing her tired shoulder muscles. "Everything is so green and lush."

"And quiet," her father added, sipping from his canteen. "It's as though there's not another person in the whole world besides us. Well, except for that fisherman."

Josh followed Mr. Wharton's pointing hand into the distance, but he couldn't discern anything that looked like a person. Only when the man suddenly moved, jerking sharply on a fishing pole, did Josh spot him.

"Looks as if he hooked one," Alicia commented. She turned to Josh. "Too bad you didn't bring your pole. You might have landed some lunch for us from that same stream."

Josh was still too upset to comment, so he just watched the angler trying to land the fish.

Suddenly, Mr. Wharton pointed again. "Look! There's a bear in the brush behind that man!"

Josh looked, but he couldn't see anything except the fisherman and the silver splashes of water thrown up by the fighting fish.

"Yes," Alicia agreed. "A black bear." Again she turned to Josh. "See him?"

Josh momentarily forgot his concern about Tank. He looked away from the fisherman just as his line went slack, showing that the fish had gotten away. "No, I don't see a bear."

Alicia started to point, then stopped. "I've lost him. Dad, where did he go?"

"Vanished into the brush." Mr. Wharton replaced his canteen on his belt. "Come on. We'd better warn that fisherman."

Hurrying down the trail toward the stream, Alicia remarked, "Now, Josh, you know why we whistle or talk or make noise when we're hiking in Alaska. This is real bear country."

Josh nodded without replying. In his short time here, he had already encountered a young black bear and a monster grizzly. Like other kids he knew, he carried bear spray, even when venturing into the wooded area behind his home in the small community of Fireweed.*

The trio reached the bottom of the hill and started picking their way along the stream. Josh watched his feet to avoid tripping over stones, and his thoughts returned to his best friend.

The three hikers rounded a moraine* that was as big as a small hill and came upon a second fisherman in hip waders who had previously been hidden from view. He glanced up from where he was crouched on shore, changing flies from a Black Gnat to a Royal Coachman.

"Hi," he said, straightening up. "I didn't hear you coming."

Josh realized the speaker was a boy about his own age. Alicia noticed, too, for she flashed a big smile. "Any luck?" she asked, keeping the smile going and moving close to approach the boy.

"Just got here a few minutes ago," he replied. He nodded his bare head toward the other fisherman, who was about a hundred yards upstream and had his back to the others. "My dad just lost one, though."

Mr. Wharton nodded and said, "Yes, we watched from up on the hill. We were heading down to alert him that there was a bear in the bush behind him."

"Bears are everywhere," the boy said casually. "But maybe I'd better go tell Dad." He shifted his gaze to Josh and asked, "You a fly fisherman?"

"I've done some," Josh admitted, studying the other boy. He was about Josh's height but heavier by several pounds. Dark brown eyes peered out from a full, round face.

"I fish, too," Alicia said. "My dad here owns some lake lodges, so we fly in where the really big ones are."

Josh flinched at Alicia's implied suggestion that the other boy was fishing for minnows when whales could be caught elsewhere.

"There are some pretty good-sized rainbows in this stream," the boy replied stiffly, obviously somewhat insulted. He added quickly, "You want to try?" and extended the light fly rod toward Alicia.

"No, thanks," she said, apparently above fishing for small

fry. "But Josh might. He's new to Alaska."

Josh glanced at her in annoyance. He wasn't in a fishing mood.

"A cheechako,* huh?" the boy asked with a hint of disapproval. "Well, we can't all be lucky enough to be born here." He extended the rod to Josh. "Here, take this while I run down and tell my dad about that bear. Catch a fish while I'm gone."

Taken off guard, Josh protested, "I don't have a license."

"Don't need one," Alicia said quickly. "Anyone under 14 in Alaska can fish without it. Go ahead, Josh. Catch one. I want to change my boots. These are wearing a blister on my heel."

Her father nodded. "Why not, Josh?" he asked. "You'll help this young man out and give all of us a chance to rest before we go on to climb that mountain."

"Thanks," the boy said, almost forcing the rod into Josh's reluctant hands. "It's all ready. I'll be right back."

Before Josh could protest further, the other boy turned and began clumping along the bank in his clumsy waders.

"Go ahead," Alicia urged. "Cast it out there, Josh."

Josh obeyed, first checking the dry fly to make sure it was securely fastened to the line. Then, standing back from the shore so he wouldn't scare the fish, he stripped off line with his left hand, brought the rod tip back with his right, and snapped it forward.

Alicia clapped her hands gleefully like a little child. "Good one, Josh!" she squealed. "Now just let it settle . . ."

Josh felt a rush of annoyance at being told how to fish, but he kept quiet and watched the fly settle gently onto the water's surface.

Almost immediately, the water exploded as a fish struck. The rod tip bent sharply. Josh felt a surge of excitement as the fish darted away.

"You got one!" Alicia exclaimed. "A big one, too! Careful now! Don't lose him!"

Josh felt such exhilaration at the unexpected strike that he didn't mind Alicia's unwanted coaching. He concentrated on playing the fish, careful to keep the line taut so it wouldn't throw the hook, but not so tight that the line would be broken.

Mr. Wharton called out, "You're doing great! You're going to land this one, Josh!"

Josh wasn't sure about that, but he was going to do his best. He ignored Alicia's constant stream of advice and tried to remember all he had learned in previous years of fishing. That included remaining calm, but his heart was racing with excitement as the fish tired and slowly allowed itself to be pulled toward the bank.

"You've done it!" Alicia shouted a moment later when Josh lifted the rod tip and an 18-inch-long trout struggled in the air above the water. "Better grab him," she warned. "Without a net, he could flop back into the water!"

Josh was so excited that he gave the rod tip a sharp jerk. That sent the fish sailing in a silvery arc away from the river and off to the right, about 10 feet from where Josh stood.

"Grab him!" Alicia commanded as the trout bounced around on the ground.

As he moved toward the fish, Josh juggled the rod in one hand and reached down with the other to seize his prize.

"Hurry up!" Alicia screamed as the fish flopped wildly.

"I'm trying!" Josh cried just as he slid his forefinger into the gills. Lifting the prize triumphantly, Josh exclaimed, "Got him!"

Alicia yelled, "Hang on to—" She broke off as a sudden crashing sound came from the brush, and her eyes turned and then fearfully opened wide at what she saw.

Josh spun around to see a large black bear charging toward him. The surprised boy took a couple of quick steps backward, then tripped over a stone and fell hard on his back, the fish still in his hand.

The next moment, the bear was standing over Josh, growling and baring long teeth just inches from the boy's terrified face!

Chapter Two

A FRIENDSHIP IN PERIL

Everything happened so fast that it didn't seem real to Josh. He lay without moving while the bear stood over him, growling deep in its huge chest. Vicious teeth clicked horribly above Josh's face. A sickening wild-animal stench from the open mouth nearly gagged him. The many stories he had heard about severe Alaskan bear maulings streaked through Josh's mind.

Dimly, as from a great distance, he heard Mr. Wharton shout, "Don't move! Play dead! I'm going to use my spray on him, so close your eyes!"

Numbly Josh obeyed. He vaguely recalled reading that sometimes a bear didn't press an attack if the victim offered no resistance. Josh tried not to move a muscle, though he knew his right hand was twitching. Then he realized that it was the trout trying to escape from where Josh had his finger in its gills.

"He wants the fish!" Alicia shouted. "Let it go!"

Josh straightened his finger and felt the fish slide free. Instantly the bear swiped at the trout, the sharp claws raking Josh's outstretched arm in the process.

Josh still didn't move, quickly recalling stories of how bears had left a victim, only to turn and renew the attack when the animal saw movement. Josh couldn't resist opening his eyes, however, even after Mr. Wharton's warning about the bear spray. Lying flat on his back, Josh saw Mr. Wharton rush toward the animal with the spray can extended in his right hand.

Turning only his eyes, Josh saw a stream of spray flying at the bear's eyes and the mouth that now held the trout. An anguished roar ripped from the bear's shaggy throat. It dropped the fish, then spun around and crashed into the brush, bawling loudly.

"You hurt?" Mr. Wharton asked anxiously, dropping the spray can and bending over Josh.

"I don't think so," Josh answered as he sat up and checked his arm. "Skinned up a little is all."

Alicia exclaimed, "Daddy grabbed his spray right away, but he couldn't get a clear shot at the bear's face until—"

She was interrupted by the other boy, who dashed up with his father. "You all right?" they asked together. "We saw what happened."

Josh nodded and got to his feet, with Mr. Wharton reaching out to help him. "Just scared out of a year's growth is all," Josh said with a grin.

The other boy's relief turned to anger. "You dumb cheechako!" he exclaimed. "Why didn't you give up the fish?"

"Easy, Tyler," his father urged. He was a big man with a flushed face. He wore hip waders, a fishing vest, and a crushed hat decorated with colorful flies.

Josh stared in surprise at the other boy, who glared at Josh as though the whole incident were his fault.

"I'm sorry about all this," the other man said, lightly brushing some dirt from Josh's shoulders. "The same thing happened to my son here a few weeks ago."

"It did?" Josh exclaimed.

"Sure did," the other boy replied, "but I had sense enough to let go of the fish. The bear ran off with it."

Josh rankled, and Tyler's father grabbed his arm and gave it a warning squeeze. Josh didn't say anything but wondered why the boy who had loaned him the fishing rod and urged him to try his luck was now acting so mean.

"I'm Charley Radburn," the other man said, extending his right hand to Alicia's father. "He's Tyler."

When introductions had been completed all around, Mr. Radburn explained, "We reported the attack on Tyler to the Alaska State Police, who told the park rangers and fish and wildlife officers."

"Didn't do much good, though," Tyler said.

"You can't blame them," his father replied. "They really tried to find that bear. After this attack, though, they'll have no choice but to track it down."

"You mean kill it?" Josh asked.

"Naw," Tyler sneered. "They shoot a dart into the bear and tranquilize it with some kind of drug. Then they fly the bear far away so that it won't come back."

Alicia nodded. "I've heard about that and seen it done on

TV nature shows," she said. "The drug wears off, and the bear doesn't suffer any lasting effects."

"Well," Alicia's father said, "time's getting away from us. Josh, instead of hiking on to that mountain, I think we should go back and have your arm looked after."

"It's all right, Mr. Wharton," Josh assured him. "Let's just use a first-aid kit and—"

"I don't mean to butt in," Mr. Radburn interrupted, "but I'd suggest seeing a doctor. You don't want to risk getting an infection."

"That makes sense," Mr. Wharton agreed. "Let's go back."

After a moment's hesitation, Josh agreed. The two men shook hands, and Josh thanked Tyler for letting him use the pole. The other boy didn't speak aloud, but Josh saw his lips move, forming a word. Instinctively, Josh was sure it was *cheechako*.

On the hike back toward home, Josh grew curious about what Tyler had called him. "Mr. Wharton," he asked, "what does *cheechako* mean?"

"That's a newcomer, greenhorn, or inexperienced person— the opposite of a sourdough,* who's an old-timer."

Josh said, "So cheechako is sort of like a malihini* in Hawaiian."

"Not exactly," Alicia explained. "Malihini has more of a nice meaning than cheechako. Anyway, Tyler shouldn't have called you that."

"He sure did change quickly," Josh noted. Then he shrugged. "It doesn't matter. I'll never see him again." Putting

Tyler out of his mind, Josh focused on what he would say to smooth things over with Tank.

Once he got home, his mother insisted that he get medical attention for the bear claw scratches. While she was getting ready to go and Mr. Wharton and Alicia waited to drive her and Josh to the doctor, Josh went to another room and called Tank's house. His mother answered.

"Hi, Mrs. Catlett," Josh said excitedly. "I've got something really interesting to tell Tank."

"Oh, Josh, I'm sorry." Her voice sounded sincere across the line. "He said that if you called, I was to tell you that he doesn't feel like talking."

Josh swallowed hard before answering, "But I've got to speak to him."

"What happened between you two boys?"

"Didn't Tank tell you?"

"No, but he said enough that I can guess this girl, Alicia, is somehow involved. Can you tell me?"

"I . . . I'd rather not."

"I don't like this," Mrs. Catlett said firmly. "You boys always get along so well."

"Oh, we've had a couple of quarrels over the years, but I didn't think this time it was anything important. I guess Tank does."

"Apparently so. He came home very distressed."

Josh flinched, sorry that his best friend was so upset. Josh pleaded, "Please, Mrs. Catlett, ask Tank to come to the phone."

"I told you, he said he doesn't want to."

"But I've got to talk to him! Please?"

"I'm sorry, Josh. I can't go against his wishes in this case."

Josh closed his eyes in misery and tried to decide what to do. Then he said, "Well, maybe he'll want to talk if you tell him I just had a close call with a bear—"

"A bear?" Mrs. Catlett's voice shot up anxiously. "Are you all right?"

"Yes, but Mom's taking me to the doctor—"

"Doctor?" Tank's mother interrupted with genuine concern in her tone. "What happened?"

"The bear's claws broke the skin on my arm, so Mom wants to have it checked. But I didn't get hurt otherwise."

"Thank God! You must tell me what happened. If you want, I won't tell Tank so you can when you two patch things up. But I'd like to know."

"Okay. . ." Josh briefly described his encounter with the bear, adding, "But everything ended up all right."

"What about Alicia and her father? Are they okay?"

"Oh, sure. The bear only bothered me because he seems to think it's easier to steal fish from people than to catch his own."

Mrs. Catlett paused, then lowered her voice. "I don't like you boys having something unpleasant between you. I probably shouldn't say this, but if you come over, maybe Tank will talk to you. I can't promise, though."

"Thanks. I'll be there as soon as I get back from the doctor's."

A few minutes later, a light rain had begun to fall as Josh

and his mother rode with Mr. Wharton and Alicia to the doctor's office.

Suddenly, Mrs. Ladd exclaimed, "Oh, Josh, I meant to call your father and tell him what happened."

"I'll do that while you're in with the doctor," Mr. Wharton volunteered.

"Oh, thank you, Trent," Mrs. Ladd said. "He's at his newspaper office. Tell him I'll call after we see the doctor."

"Of course," Alicia's father answered, glancing at Josh in the rearview mirror. "While you're getting treated, I'll also call the state police to report the incident."

Alicia added, "From what that boy, Tyler, and his father said, the police will call in the park rangers, and maybe fish and game department people, to try to locate that bear. Since this is at least the second attack on a person, the officers will probably want to talk to you, because now they're sure to trap and remove that bear."

"That's for certain, Josh," her father agreed, easing the car down the mountain to where the town of Fireweed was nestled in a small valley. "They'll want statements from Alicia and me, too."

Mrs. Ladd asked anxiously, "Trent, do you think they'll want Josh to go back there with the rangers and show them where it happened?"

"That sounds logical," he replied. "But don't worry. Josh won't be in any danger with that many people around. Some of them will be armed, too."

Josh asked, "Mr. Wharton, do you suppose they would let

Tank come along?"

"He's not needed!" Alicia snapped. "He wasn't there."

"No, but he could have been," Josh said, agitated at the girl's tone.

"Just the same, why do you want him along?" Alicia asked disapprovingly.

Josh clamped his jaws tightly to avoid making the sharp reply that almost sprang from his lips.

"Alicia," her father said firmly, "that's enough."

Mrs. Ladd, seeing the look on Josh's face, gave her son's hand a warning squeeze and said quietly, "That goes for you, too."

Slowly, Josh took a deep breath and brooded silently. He determined that when he got Alicia alone, he was going to insist she get along with Tank. *But,* Josh wondered, *how can I get Tank to get along with Alicia if Tank won't even speak to me?*

A few minutes later, the doctor was cleaning the bear scratches. Then the nurse bandaged Josh's arm and gave him an antibiotic shot to prevent infection.

When Josh and his mother returned to the waiting room, Mr. Wharton and Alicia each put down a magazine and stood up.

"All fixed up, Josh?" Mr. Wharton asked.

"All done," he replied. "How about the phone calls?"

"Also done," Alicia answered quickly.

Mrs. Ladd said, "I've got to call John and tell him that the doctor says Josh will be all right." She headed for the pay phone in the hallway.

When she returned after a couple of minutes, Josh told her, "Mr. Wharton called the state police, and they said the rangers and wildlife officials will definitely relocate that bear."

"They called it a nuisance bear," Mr. Wharton added. "And when I phoned your husband, he said he had been thinking about doing a story on that very subject. He's going to call the proper authorities and see if he can ride along when they fly that bear to a new location."

Josh's eyes lit up. "Wow! I'd like to go along," he said. "Mom, do you suppose Dad would let me?"

"I don't think he's the one to make that decision," Mrs. Ladd replied, stepping through the outside door that Mr. Wharton held open.

"She's right," Mr. Wharton added, motioning Alicia and Josh to follow Mrs. Ladd into the light drizzle. "That's up to the state or federal officials in charge of animal relocation."

Josh's excitement kept his hopes up. "Most people are glad to get free publicity for the good things they do," he said. "In Hawaii, I don't think Dad ever got turned down when he wanted to write a story. Sometimes I got to go along, especially after I learned to shoot video footage. Dad could take a certain frame out and use it as a still picture. Remember, Mom?"

"Yes, of course," Mrs. Ladd said. "But I'm not sure I want any member of my family riding along in an airplane with a wild bear."

Josh laughed. "Aw, Mom, he'd be tranquilized and asleep through the whole flight."

"He'd be tied down, too," Mr. Wharton added.

Mrs. Ladd shook her head. "What would happen if one of Alaska's famous storms sprang up real fast and the plane was delayed? The bear could wake up and—"

"No problem, Mom!" Josh insisted. "The plane would just land."

"That's right," Alicia agreed. "Dad, maybe I could ride along, too."

"I want Tank to come," Josh said without thinking. Then he saw from the look on Alicia's face that he had hurt her feelings. "Sorry," he said to her.

"I know Tank's your best friend," she said coldly, her eyes suddenly brighter than usual, "but he doesn't have to be your *only* friend."

Josh didn't answer, and Alicia didn't speak again, so the two adults began making casual conversation about the weather. A silent chill settled over Josh and Alicia.

Josh kept trying to think of something to say, but he couldn't. He and Alicia rode the rest of the way back to the Ladds' home in awkward silence, while Josh wondered if Tank would talk to him when Josh got to his house.

After Alicia and her father had gone, Josh pulled on a light rain jacket and walked out of his home on Sourdough Street at the corner of Skookum* Drive. He turned left, deep in thought about what to say to Tank.

Ordinarily, Josh would have enjoyed seeing some neighbor kids, but now he didn't feel like talking to anyone. He became aware of his shoes crunching on the graveled street and wished he could be quieter.

As he walked to the end of Sourdough where it turned uphill onto Clouds Rest Court, Josh remembered that Alicia had lived there before moving to Anchorage. Through a break in the trees, Josh could see that city spread out in the distance below. Josh cringed to think what it would be like if she still lived there, a block from Tank.

Turning up Clouds Rest, Josh kept a wary eye out for moose or bear on the heavily forested hillside, where Tank lived in one of the only two houses on that street.

Josh's hopes rose when he saw Tank crouched by the front steps, working on his bicycle. "Hey!" Josh cried, running toward his friend. "I got jumped by a big ol' black bear this morning!"

Tank looked up with interest. "Yeah? What happened?" he asked.

Grateful that Tank was speaking to him, Josh hurriedly explained. He concluded, ". . . and when I heard Alicia scream, I turned around and saw this blackie rushing toward me. The next thing I knew, I was down and it was standing over me, baring big teeth in my face."

"Yeah?" Tank's eyes dropped to Josh's bandaged forearm. "The bear do that to you?"

"Yes, but it was really after the fish. Mr. Wharton drove it off with bear spray." Happy that Tank was listening, Josh rushed on. "You should have been there!" he said.

Tank's voice turned cold. "I would have been, but you wanted to be with Alicia instead of me."

"That's not true!"

"No? Maybe you should spend more time with her. See how long *you* can get along with her!"

Tank turned and ran up the stairs, ignoring Josh's cries of "Wait! Wait!"

When the door slammed behind Tank, Josh closed his eyes and groaned aloud.

Chapter Three

THE BEST-LAID PLANS

Feeling hurt and confused, Josh started back toward his home. There were no sidewalks, so he walked down the middle of the graveled street.

The light June drizzle had stopped and the sun was burning through the cloud cover when he glanced across the street at Ryan Spitzer's house. Although Ryan was sometimes pugnacious and annoying, Josh liked him. Josh didn't feel like talking to anyone else right then, though. But just as he thought he was safely past Ryan's house, the front door burst open.

"Hey, wait up!" Ryan called.

Josh didn't stop but said over his shoulder, "I can't. I've got to get home."

"You see Tank?" Ryan asked, running to catch up.

Josh suppressed a sigh and slowed his pace until the other boy caught up with him. He was more than half a head taller than Ryan, who always reminded Josh of a banty rooster.* "Just left him," he said noncommittally.

Ryan's gaze dropped to Josh's bandaged arm. "What

happened? A goldfish bite you?" Ryan said, laughing at his own joke.

But Josh didn't even smile. "It's nothing," he said evasively, quickening his step.

"Tell me anyway," Ryan demanded, hurrying to keep up.

Josh sighed and briefly recounted his encounter with the bear.

Ryan shook his head. "You should have given up the fish right away," he said. "Could have saved yourself a trip to the doctor."

Josh gritted his teeth. He didn't need Ryan's usual overbearing opinion. Still, Josh managed to explain quietly, "That's what the other kid who was there said, too. But it all happened so fast. I just glimpsed the bear charging out of the brush, then suddenly I fell on my back, and it was straddling me. Believe me, with 300 pounds of growling animal snapping big teeth in my face, I didn't think of the fish."

"I would have had my spray out before ol' blackie even got to me," Ryan announced smugly. "I'd have given him a face full in half a second flat."

Josh stopped abruptly and turned to look down at the shorter boy, biting back angry words. Taking a moment to relax, he answered, "Well, you're more experienced than me." *Now, how do I get rid of Ryan?* he wondered. Josh cocked his head as though listening and asked, "Is that your mother calling you?"

"Nope. She and my sisters went shopping." Ryan quickly added, "What was the name of that other kid?"

"Tyler Radburn."

"Oh, Ty Radburn."

"His father called him Tyler. You know him?"

"Do I?" Ryan made a snorting noise. "I wish I didn't."

Something about Ryan's obvious dislike for the other boy made Josh glad that he never expected to see Tyler again. "What's the matter with him?" he asked.

"He thinks he knows everything just because he was born in Alaska and most of us came here from other states." Ryan thrust out his chin in a pugnacious manner that Josh had come to recognize as a habit. "He's a know-it-all!" Ryan said contemptuously. "That's what's the matter with Ty."

Josh could barely suppress a smile. "Some guys are like that, Ryan," he said.

"He's the only one I know."

Josh's smile almost got away from him before he recovered enough to ask, "Where do you know him from?"

"School. He's in my class. You and Tank will get to know him this fall."

Josh's smile vanished, and a groan escaped his lips.

"What's the matter?" Ryan asked. "Your arm hurt?"

"It's not important," Josh said grimly. He had been looking forward to his first year in Alaska's public schools. But now, suddenly, he wished he could be home-schooled like Jacob Ashton or attend a Christian school like Luke Gulley—anything that would keep him away from Tyler Radburn.

Ryan asked, "Was Tank there when the bear jumped you?"

"No."

"Why not?" Ryan persisted.

Josh stopped and scowled at Ryan. "I don't want to talk about it."

The other boy nodded knowingly. "Had a fight, huh?"

"No, we didn't! I gotta go." Josh sprinted down the street, leaving his pesky questioner behind.

A few minutes later, he was back at the Ladds' white home. It faced green mountains rising 4,000 feet, less than a quarter mile away. For environmental reasons, the house had a small "footprint" and wasn't spread out like ranch-style homes. Instead, this one was built into a mountainside so it took up little space. It appeared from the front to be only one story tall, but it had a lower bedroom floor with large windows in each room. These had sliding glass doors that opened to a tiny strip of back lawn that backed up against a greenbelt.*

Josh threw himself face down on his bed and then turned to stare gloomily out the window. His mother entered from his little brother's bedroom with a hamper full of laundry.

"You want to talk?" she asked, standing by the foot of Josh's bed.

"No, thanks, Mom."

"I'll be here if you change your mind," she said. Then she returned to the other bedroom with her hamper.

Josh again stared through the window, past spruce, cottonwood, and aspen trees growing just outside. He didn't notice Skyline Loop, the main paved street below, which threaded down the forest-covered mountain to the small business district on the valley floor by Glenn Highway. Absently, Josh lifted his gaze to a marvelous view of several mountain ranges in the distance. But his thoughts were entirely on Tank.

After several minutes, he sat up, a decision made. "Mom," he finally called, "I'm going back to Tank's house."

A short while later, Josh knocked on the Catletts' door, determined to talk the situation out with Tank. Josh was glad when Tank answered the door instead of his mother.

"We've got to talk," Josh said quickly before Tank could close the door.

"We have nothing to talk about."

"I came to say I'm sorry for what happened back there on the trail."

Tank took a slow, deep breath before answering. Then he said, "You said I was silly. That hurt my feelings, Josh."

"I didn't say *you* were silly. You said that Alicia was always talking to me and ignoring you. I said *that* was silly, but I shouldn't have said even that."

"You thought it, so you said it." Tank's tone revealed his suppressed anger.

"We've been friends too long to let something like this come between us," Josh insisted.

"Not some *thing*," Tank snapped, "but that *girl!*"

"We've talked about Alicia, so I thought you understood her. I mean, her mother died, she's got no brothers or sisters, and she's used to getting her own way. But deep down, I think she's a nice person who just doesn't know how to make friends."

"Well, let her find other friends besides you."

"I'm sure she wants to be your friend, too, but you won't let her."

"Yeah, that's right. I want to keep it that way, too."

Josh paused, then said thoughtfully, "I just wish you two could get along."

"That's easy! Make her stay away from us!"

Josh sighed softly and fell silent. He realized he wasn't making any progress on that subject, but he was glad that at least Tank was talking to him.

Tank's gaze dropped to Josh's bandaged forearm, then lifted again to meet Josh's eyes. "Does it hurt much?" he asked.

"No, the bear's claws just raked my skin."

"Too bad it didn't happen to Alicia instead."

"This isn't like you, Tank," Josh said in mild reproof. "You wouldn't really want her to be hurt like that."

"There you go again!" Tank's eyes flashed with anger. "You're taking her side!"

"I'm not taking anybody's—"

"We have nothing else to say to each other!" Tank interrupted. He quickly stepped back inside and slammed the door.

Josh stood for a moment, completely miserable. Slowly, with a heavy heart, he turned and walked toward home.

On the way, he met Jacob Ashton and his malamute, Williwaw.* The large, wolflike sled dog with the cap-and-mask face rushed toward Josh, barking wildly. Josh stopped to pet the animal while Jacob came running up.

"Ryan tells me you got scratched by a bear," Jacob said by

way of greeting.

Josh didn't feel like talking, so he didn't stop, but he did hold up his bandaged arm and say, "It's nothing serious."

Jacob snapped his fingers and commanded, "Willi, heel." When the dog obeyed, coming to the boy's left side, they fell into step with Josh. "How did it happen?" he asked.

Josh tried to discourage further conversation so he could get home and be alone to think. "Didn't Ryan tell you?" he said.

"Yes, but I want to hear it from you."

"Look, Jacob, I'm just not in the mood. Okay?"

"Okay." Jacob's voice held a hint of disappointment. The boys had reached the chain link fence with the four-foot-high hedge in front of Josh's home. Jacob added, "I know it must have been real scary to have that bear standing over you, but still, I sort of feel sorry for the bear."

Josh stopped in surprise. "You do?" he said.

"Sure. We get bears like him every once in a while. He's learned that it's easier to let people catch his fish than to do it himself. Because he scares people, he'll be tranquilized and flown far away. There he'll have to adjust to new surroundings, and there probably won't be any fishermen to rob. I hope he can learn to survive."

"He's a wild animal, Jacob. He'll survive."

"Probably, but how would you feel if you were suddenly taken away from everything that's familiar and had to survive in a strange environment all by yourself?"

Josh shook his head. "You've got an interesting way of

thinking," he said. "Well, see you later, Jacob." Josh moved toward the front door.

Jacob called after him, "Think about it."

There was no time to do that, however, because when he entered the house, his mother met him. "Your father called," she said. "He talked to both the forest rangers and the Alaska fish and wildlife people about that bear. Somebody will be out to question you about your encounter."

"Good! I'll be here." Josh started downstairs to his bedroom, but his mother continued.

"There's more," she said.

Josh stopped on the stairs and looked back up at her. She explained, "Your father talked to the officials about doing a story on how a nuisance bear is relocated after being tranquilized. Your father is going to ride along to where the bear is re-released."

"Wow! I'd like to go too, Mom. You think Dad will let me?"

"It's not up to him, you know."

"He could get permission from the right people for me to fly along. I could take my video camera—"

"Not so fast, Josh!" she protested. "I'm not at all eager for you to be in a plane with a wild animal."

"Aw, Mom!" Josh broke in. "You worry too much!"

"And some boys don't realize they're not invincible, even though they sometimes think they are."

"Nothing's going to happen, Mom. So if Dad can get permission, is it okay with you if I go on that trip?"

His mother regarded him in thoughtful silence before answering, "I guess so, if your father approves."

Things moved quickly after that. Josh went with the officials to show them where the bear incident had occurred. After he returned home, he vainly tried again to think of a way to convince Tank and Alicia to get along.

Over the next couple of days, Mr. Ladd obtained permission from the authorities for Josh to join the team when the bear was relocated. Josh waited impatiently for news that the bear had been found and tranquilized.

On the third day, Josh's father called home from his Anchorage office. "Son," he began, "they've got the bear and right now are waiting for a helicopter to lift him out of the park in a sling. They'll take him to Lake Hood and transfer him to a big float plane. In a few hours, that bear will be far away at a new home in some remote part of Alaska."

"Are you coming home to take me out to the lake?" Josh asked.

"I've got a problem, Son. Something's come up here at work, and I can't go."

"Oh, Dad!" Josh groaned.

"Don't sound so disappointed! I promised the rangers and wildlife people I'd do a story. If you'll go along and shoot video footage, I can use that to write my piece."

"I'll do a good job, Dad!"

"I know you will. Ordinarily, I wouldn't risk letting you go without my being along, but a friend of mine, Herb Dabney, is the pilot on the float plane. He said he would look after you."

Josh's voice shot up in excitement. "Great, Dad!" he said. "I've got to hang up now and get ready."

His father chuckled. Then he said, "Shouldn't you ask when and where to meet the plane, and how I plan to get you there?"

Josh, chagrined, answered, "Of course. Go ahead and tell me."

After getting instructions, Josh rushed into the kitchen to tell his mother. She was obviously less enthusiastic than he, but Josh didn't mind. At least she had said he could go.

"I've got to call Tank," Josh announced, heading for the phone. He picked it up, then hesitated. Even if Tank talked to him, it might hurt Tank's feelings to not be able to go along on the plane.

Slowly, Josh replaced the phone, realizing that this was the first time he had done anything really interesting without his lifelong friend at his side. "Sorry, Tank," he whispered, heading downstairs to his bedroom. "I wish we could be together. It could be a great adventure."

Chapter Four

EMERGENCY IN THE SKY

Tank couldn't remember the last time he had felt so unhappy. For two days, he had brooded alone in his room. First, his mother vainly tried to persuade him to call Josh. Then she urged him to go see what Ryan, Jacob, and Luke were doing, but he wouldn't. Late on the morning of the third day, Mrs. Catlett knocked on Tank's bedroom door.

"Come in," he said dully. Still in his pajamas, he turned from where he was propped up in bed with extra pillows. A book lay at his side, but he hadn't been reading. Instead, he had been gazing out the window at the forested mountain.

Tank, being new to Alaska, hadn't yet explored the pristine wilderness. He wanted to, because neighbor boys had told him that the area was home to such wild animals as bears, wolves, and Dall sheep. But it wasn't wise to go alone, and Tank was still angry at Josh, so Tank moped in solitary misery.

His mother came over to stand beside the bed. She placed both hands on her hips in a gesture that made Tank stir uneasily. She spoke gently but firmly.

"This is no way to spend your days," she said. "I talked it over with your father before he left for work this morning, and we agreed it's time for us to intervene."

Tank waited for her to explain, but she didn't until he asked, "Yeah?"

"Unless you snap out of this and make up with Josh, I'm going to take you to the doctor. Maybe there's something physically wrong."

"I don't need a doctor!" Tank swung his legs over the side of the bed and stood up to face her. "I'm fine! I just want to be left alone."

"I'm sorry, but this has gone on long enough. Now either you get dressed and start acting like a normal boy or you're going to the doctor."

Tank took a deep breath and slowly let it out before answering, "All right. I'll go outside."

"To make up with Josh?"

"No! I don't want to see him, Mom. I'll go exploring with Jacob and Ryan or somebody, but not Josh."

"I think that's a mistake, but I'll respect your decision." Mrs. Catlett turned toward the door, then stopped. "Oh, by the way, Mary Ladd called. She said that Josh is going to fly with a tranquilized bear that's being relocated. I thought you'd like to know."

Tank closed his eyes in disappointment, then quickly recovered. "I don't care," he said without conviction.

But he did care, and when his mother left the room, Tank slammed his fist down hard against the pillow. As he showered and dressed, his mood grew darker. In spite of his best efforts, he kept thinking about Josh, wishing he could be with him as they relocated the wild bear.

* * *

Several miles away, Josh stood beside Lake Hood Air Harbor near Anchorage International Airport. He closed his left eye and looked with the right through the viewfinder on his video camera. He began taking slow panning shots of the activity at the world's largest and busiest seaplane base. One after another, small float aircraft landed on or took off from the water.

An air of excitement surrounded Josh as he carefully eased the camera down to rest on a large twin-engine seaplane secured to the dock in front of him. He pressed the camera's zoom button to widen the shot. The entire plane, with floats under each side of the high single wing, was neatly framed in the viewfinder when he pushed the start button.

Herb Dabner, the tall, middle-aged pilot, completed his preflight check and came over to stand beside Josh. "They're about to load the bear, in case you want to get shots of that," Mr. Dabner said.

"Sure do," Josh agreed. He quickly turned off the camera. In a glance, he saw several men standing around the same large black bear that had taken Josh's fish a few days before. The animal was quiet from the effects of the tranquilizer drug.

Josh returned the camera to his eye and recorded the men

easing the animal from a flat, wheeled cart. The camera whirred quietly as they slid the bear through the cargo door located about two-thirds of the way back from the wing.

When the men and beast disappeared inside the plane, Josh pressed the stop button. "Got it, Mr. Dabner," he said.

"Your dad will be proud," Mr. Dabner replied. "Well, they'll have 'Mr. Bruin,' our bear, securely tied down in just a few minutes. We'll be on our way as soon as the copilot arrives."

Josh looked around the grounds behind him and said, "I hope he makes it soon. I'd hate to have that bear wake up before we get to where we're going to release it."

Mr. Dabner smiled reassuringly. "I don't think that's going to be a problem. It's only a 45-minute flight, and here comes the copilot. But who's that with him?"

Josh followed the pilot's pointing arm. "Tyler Radburn!" he exclaimed. "I don't believe this!"

"You know him, Josh?"

"I've met him," Josh replied shortly. He thought about describing his unpleasant experience with the other boy but decided to keep quiet. Still, he felt his stomach tighten as Tyler and the other man approached.

"Ross," the pilot said, "this is Josh Ladd. I'm a friend of his father. Josh, shake hands with Ross Ashby, a park ranger and as fine a copilot as I ever flew with."

Shaking hands with the man, Josh kept his eyes on Tyler Radburn. Tyler stared back, his lips silently forming a word. Josh was sure it was *cheechako*.

Mr. Ashby introduced the other boy. "This is my nephew, Ty Radburn. He's going along with us if nobody minds."

Josh minded very much, but he didn't say anything, and neither did Tyler. He looked scornfully at Josh, and his upper right lip curled in a sneer that the men didn't notice. Josh silently wished that Tank were here with him instead of Tyler.

One of the uniformed men inside the plane stuck his head out the open cargo door. "All secure in here," he said. "We're ready when you fly boys are."

The copilot motioned Josh to precede him and Tyler through the cargo door and into the plane's interior. From the outside, the aircraft had seemed fairly large. But with the bear tied down in the center of the floor, and four men and two boys occupying the remaining space, the interior seemed small. It was also filled with the rank stench of a wild animal.

The copilot in his ranger's uniform headed toward the front, saying, "There are no passenger seats, so Ty and Josh, you make yourselves as comfortable as possible against the left bulkhead. I'll be up front in the cockpit."

Josh was relieved to notice that all the men except the pilot wore holstered pistols. Josh was even more relieved when the armed and uniformed fish and game officer slid down to sit on the floor between him and Tyler.

"I'm Ned Blenker," he said, stretching his long legs toward the helpless bear. "I guess you boys won't mind me being a tiny bit closer to this big fellow than you are."

"Not at all," Josh confessed with a smile. He was glad to have someone between him and Tyler.

Mr. Blenker jerked his chin toward the second park ranger. He was settling down directly opposite them on the other side of the bear. "He's Chester Tobias," Mr. Blenker said. "He and Ross, the copilot, work together."

Mr. Dabner turned from his place on the right front side of the cockpit. There was a small window to his right. "All set back there?" he called.

When everyone nodded, the pilot glanced over at Mr. Ashby. He had strapped himself into the copilot's seat on the left, below another small window. He nodded, and the pilot began turning over the first engine.

It coughed in coming to life, then began to run smoothly. The sound and vibration filled the plane's interior. Josh lifted his video camera and began filming a wide shot, taking in the bear and the plane's occupants.

"Hey!" Tyler exclaimed, scowling and leaning forward to speak across the officer sitting between them. "I don't like having my picture taken."

Josh immediately hit the stop button. "Sorry," he said, lowering the camera. "My dad's in the newspaper business, and I promised him I'd document this flight. You'll probably have your name in the paper when the story comes out."

"Then we'll all be famous," Mr. Blenker said heartily, reaching out to put his arms over both boys' shoulders. "Everybody in Alaska will know our names. Won't that be great?"

Tyler's scowl slid away. "I guess that's all right," he said. "Go ahead and shoot your old pictures."

Josh lifted the camera and zoomed in to get close-ups of each person, though he got only the back of the pilot's and copilot's heads. Then he reversed the zoom for a wide shot on the bear.

Through the viewfinder, Josh noticed that the animal's mouth and eyes were open. As Josh zoomed in for a close-up of the long fangs, a low, threatening growl rumbled from the bear.

Josh raised his voice to be heard above the roaring of the second engine, which had also begun to run. "Any chance of that bear coming to before we get to where we're going to drop him off?" he asked Mr. Blenker.

"Don't worry, Josh," Mr. Blenker said somberly. "He's been given just enough drug to keep him immobilized until we release him. He needs to be pretty much ready to come out of it by then. We wouldn't want to leave him until we're sure he's going to be all right."

Josh nodded. "I have a hunch he's going to be mighty unhappy when that drug wears off, so I wouldn't want to be anywhere near him when that happens."

"Me either," the fish and game officer agreed. "He might resent all that we've had to do to him." Mr. Blenker laced his fingers behind his head and closed his eyes as the plane began taxiing on the lake's surface.

Moments later, they were airborne and over the body of water known as Knik Arm.* The plane passed through low clouds before the twin engines settled down into a steady, almost hypnotic sound. Soon Josh fell asleep.

He was awakened a while later by a sickening lurch of the airplane. Josh opened his eyes and glanced at the cockpit in alarm.

The pilot twisted in his seat and caught Josh's eye. "Just a little turbulence," he called above the engine noise. The plane continued to bounce as the pilot added, "There's some stormy weather moving in ahead of us. We're going to climb over it. We may experience some chop.*"

That was an understatement, Josh decided in the next few minutes as the plane was buffeted and the weather worsened. Josh glanced at the fish and game officer beside him. Mr. Blenker was still asleep, his boots just inches from the bear's half-open mouth.

Lifting his gaze, Josh noticed with satisfaction that Tyler was sitting up straight, his face tight and gray. *Well,* Josh told himself, *I think he's more concerned than I am.*

Josh looked across the bear's still, shaggy form to where Mr. Tobias, the second ranger, was being bounced around.

He caught Josh's eye and forced a smile. "Wish I'd brought my spurs to ride this baby," he said cheerfully.

Josh tried to return the smile but wasn't very successful. He called toward the cockpit, where he could see heavy rain on the windshield, "How are we doing?"

The pilot turned his head. "This weather is too high to fly over," he said. "We're going to try going around it."

Josh watched the plane tilt sharply, which caused the bear's weight to shift against the ropes. The bear growled ominously. Out of the corner of his eye, Josh saw Tyler jerk his feet back tight against his body. Instinctively, Josh slowly pulled his own feet back, making sure his concern wasn't evident to Tyler.

The bouncing became worse over the next several minutes, which seemed more like hours. With each severe downward plunge, Josh noticed that the bear was showing more and more signs of throwing off the effects of the drug.

Clearing his throat, Josh nudged the fish and game officer sitting between him and Tyler. "How much longer do you think that drug will last?" he asked.

Mr. Blenker didn't reply but leaned forward to examine the bear. Its eyes moved, and a deep, menacing growl came from the great, shaggy chest.

"Hey," Mr. Blenker called to the cockpit crew, "we need to land so we can get this fellow out of here before much longer."

"We're trying," the pilot called over his shoulder while his hands and feet vainly worked to keep the aircraft steady.

"Trying's not good enough," Mr. Tobias said soberly from the other side of the bear. "You'd better find a hole in those clouds and get us on the ground."

"You mean water," Tyler said. "This is a float plane."

"Water or land, it doesn't matter to me," Mr. Tobias said, checking the tie-down ropes across the bear's big body. "But it needs to be soon."

Josh licked his suddenly dry lips before asking, "Could you give him another shot?"

"Yes, but that would mean he would take much longer to

come out of it. We want to be sure he's up and able to take care of himself before we leave him."

Josh started to lean back again just as the bottom seemed to drop out from under him. The plane plummeted in a sickening drop that sent Josh's heart up to his mouth. He tried to swallow, but the lump wouldn't go away, and the plane continued its downward plunge.

Tyler yelled toward the cockpit, "What's happening, Uncle Ross?"

For a moment, neither pilot nor copilot answered. They were obviously too busy trying to keep the aircraft aloft while also peering anxiously through the windshield for a break in the clouds.

"There!" Mr. Ashby exclaimed, pointing through his left windshield. "A hole!"

"I see it." The pilot banked the plane sharply to the left. He lifted his voice so the passengers in back could hear him. "We're passing over heavily forested land toward a big lake. We're only flying at about a hundred feet or so. Get ready for landing. It may be a little rough, so hang on."

Mr. Dabner's voice was calm, but Josh sensed the man's excitement. Josh removed the camera strap from around his neck so it couldn't twist and strangle him if the landing were bumpy.

The copilot called, "We just passed over a big grizzly on the beach. Now we're over the lake, heading toward three big islands."

"Fifty feet!" the pilot called as the plane started to level out. "I'm going to try setting down close to the mainland."

Just as Josh glanced at the bear, it raised its head and began to struggle against the ropes.

Suddenly, the plane's gliding descent ended with the nose thrusting itself downward at a steep angle. The pilot yelled, "Brace your—"

Josh didn't hear the rest because the plane seemed to slam into a stone wall when it struck the water. The aircraft skidded forward. Josh was thrown around as the tail end of the aircraft tipped sharply upward.

Josh landed on the bear, its coarse, stinking hair filling his open mouth. The animal growled and tried to lift its massive head. Josh scrambled wildly to get away, but he seemed to be falling upward toward the ceiling. He realized the plane was tipping over. The tail section tipped higher, then flopped over. Slowly, everything settled, then stopped.

Josh found himself on his back, staring in surprise at the bear. It was now directly overhead. What had been the floor was now the ceiling. Ropes that had held down the tranquilized bear now sagged ominously under its weight.

"We're upside down!" Josh cried, aware that water was rushing into the plane and that the bear was coming out of its drugged state. It began to move, causing one of the ropes to break. Gravity took over, and other ropes popped rapidly.

"Oh, no!" Josh cried. He started to roll aside as the last rope split and the bear fell toward him!

Chapter Five

TEST FOR THE SURVIVORS

Talking to Jacob Ashton in front of his house, Tank suddenly jerked as though he had received an electric shock.

"What's the matter?" Jacob asked anxiously.

Tank didn't answer, but a strange feeling was sweeping over him.

"Tell me!" Jacob said sharply. "What happened?"

Slowly, as though waking from a dream, Tank turned his eyes upon the other boy. "I . . . I don't know. I just had a kind of funny feeling."

"Like what?"

Tank frowned. "I'm not sure, but it had something to do with Josh."

"What about him?"

Shaking his head, Tank replied, "I . . . don't know. I can't explain it, but I . . . I think he's in some kind of trouble."

"How could you know that? You told me a couple of minutes ago that he's miles away, flying a tranquilized bear to a relocation spot."

"I know! I know!" Tank said impatiently. He paused, then

added, "It was probably nothing." He forced a little laugh. "Just my imagination, I guess."

The sound of a car turning off Skookum Drive onto Sourdough Street made both boys turn. "Here comes Alicia with her father," Jacob said.

"Yeah, I saw them. I've got to go." Tank turned away and headed toward his home, but he stopped when the sedan pulled up beside him.

"Hi, Tank," Alicia said, opening her door and stepping onto the street. "I want to talk to you."

"We've got nothing to talk about," he said bluntly and started walking away.

"Yes, we do!" Alicia hurried to catch up with him. "Don't be difficult, Tank!"

"Difficult? Me?" he cried, stopping to face her. His eyes flashed with anger. "Josh and I have been best friends since we were babies—until you came along!"

"I realize that, but you need to listen to me."

Tank glanced beyond Alicia to where her father was talking to Jacob through the open car window. Tank turned his angry gaze back to the girl. "Don't tell me what to do," he snapped, walking away briskly.

Alicia followed. "I came all the way from Anchorage to say that I'm sorry about what happened the other day," she said. "I don't want to come between you and Josh, I just want to be friends with both of you!"

"You be his friend, but not mine. Now, stop following me!"

Tank broke into a jog and left Alicia standing in the street.

He tried to convince himself that he had really told her off, but that didn't help him feel any better. He still couldn't shake the strange feeling he'd had about Josh.

* * *

In the upside-down airplane, Josh frantically rolled aside just as the 300-pound bear fell heavily beside him in a tangle of broken ropes. Its huge mouth opened, and a guttural growl warned Josh that the tranquilizer drug was rapidly wearing off.

Without thinking, Josh dropped his video camera and scooted crablike to one side, out of the animal's reach. He tried to stand, but that wasn't easy because the plane's ceiling had not been designed for human feet. The sound of water rushing in warned Josh that the aircraft was sinking.

Mr. Tobias adjusted his revolver holster and stepped around the bear to face Josh. "You all right?" he asked.

"I think so. What happened to the plane?"

"Probably got caught in a down draft. It flipped us over. Come on. Let's get out of here before it sinks."

The pilot called, "Anybody hurt?"

Josh glanced toward the cockpit. The pilot had a bloody gash on his forehead, but it didn't seem to bother him. When everyone shouted "No," he commanded, "One of you men grab some life jackets and whatever survival gear you can reach in the tail section. Then all of you jump into that water and swim for shore—the boys first!"

"Wait!" The copilot's voice stopped everyone in the back of the plane. Mr. Ashby's face was pale, and he held both hands over his chest as though it hurt. He asked, "Ty, are you all right?"

"I think so, Uncle Ross."

Mr. Blenker spoke up. "I'll look after him, Ross. You'd better get out. The water's coming in fast—"

"In a minute," the pilot interrupted. "Josh, you sure you're okay?"

"Scratched up and banged about is all, Mr. Dabner."

"Good. Tobias, will you look after him while I help Ross? He's hurt worse than any of us, I think."

"Sure thing," Mr. Tobias replied. He tugged on Josh's arm. "Let's get out of here."

Carefully, Josh stepped around the great black mass of bear that was now raising its head and making rumbling sounds deep in its chest. With Mr. Tobias's arm steadying him, Josh moved toward the rear.

He realized that the two heavy motors were forcing the plane's nose down and the tail up, impeding their escape. They were all forced to get down on their hands and knees to climb up toward the cargo door, which had popped open when the plane hit the water. Through it, Josh could see low overcast skies and light rain falling.

Josh crawled past the last of the packs, coats, and other items that had fallen when the plane tipped over. He was spurred to greater speed by the warning sound of water rushing into the plane's interior.

He glanced at Tyler and saw that Mr. Blenker, the fish and game officer, was helping him toward the cargo door. Through it, Josh felt the rush of cool air filling the cabin.

As Josh neared the door, Mr. Blenker handed a bright orange life preserver to Tyler, who quickly put it on.

Mr. Tobias asked Josh, "Do you know how to put on one of those?" When he nodded, the ranger added, "Good! Grab one and get it on fast."

Mr. Blenker slipped a jacket on but didn't tie it before tossing other vests to Josh and Mr. Tobias.

"You boys stand in the door," Mr. Blenker commanded. "But don't jump until you're told. When we give the okay, swim straight for shore as fast as you can."

Josh and Tyler stood up on unsteady legs. They both glanced nervously at each other, then broke eye contact. Through the door, Josh scanned the dark clouds that blotted out the sun. A moderate wind made the temperature a brisk 55 to 60 degrees, he figured. He wished it was a comfortable 70 or even 80.

Struggling into his life jacket, Josh worried, *What if the plane sinks before everyone gets out safely?* He glanced back into the plane just in time to see the pilot pushing the injured copilot out the window on his side. This had been just above and to the right of his seat, but now it was on the bottom. A moment later, the pilot followed Mr. Ashby out the same window.

Mr. Tobias's voice drew Josh's attention back to the cargo doorway, where the ranger stood beside Mr. Blenker, the fish and game officer. "Boys, the water's going to be very cold. It'll be a shock, but we're only about 30 yards offshore. Swim over there as fast as you can. I'm going to see if we can salvage some of our survival gear, then I'll be right behind you boys."

"I'll help," Mr. Blenker said, shifting his weight to keep his balance as the plane lurched ominously. "Now, boys, jump away from each other and head for shore."

Tyler nodded and leaped off to his right. He let out a wild shriek as he hit the frigid water.

Josh hesitated, taking one more quick glance back into the plane. The bear was growling and trying to rise up on its front feet. Josh asked anxiously, "What about the bear?"

"It's waking up fast," Mr. Tobias replied. "I think it'll be okay. Just get out of here before it comes after us."

Josh faced the water, where Tyler was already several feet away from the plane. Taking a deep breath, Josh jumped out and away from the plane. He involuntarily gasped when he hit the incredibly cold water. It felt as if his body was instantly flash-frozen. The life jacket kept him from sinking very far, though, so he gritted his teeth and began paddling toward the willow-lined shore.

He was a strong swimmer who had often tested both California's and Hawaii's waves, but those waters were pleasant. In spite of his skill, Josh was struggling and shivering uncontrollably when he grabbed a handful of willows and pulled himself ashore a few minutes later. Gasping for breath from exertion and the cold, he turned to see Tyler already sitting in the willows.

"Made it!" Tyler yelled triumphantly. "Made it!"

"Thank God," Josh replied, his teeth chattering so much that the words were hardly distinguishable. He forced his chilled body to move up the bank to make room for the men to come ashore. But when he glanced back, he saw they were still at the plane.

The pilot was crouched on the upside-down wing, shouting through cupped hands to the two men still standing in the open cargo doorway, "She's sinking fast! Get out of there!"

Josh heard Mr. Blenker's answer. "I've got jackets for both of you," he said. "Stay there! I'll bring them . . ."

He broke off and turned to look inside the plane. Then, with a frightened yell, he leaped into the water with two life jackets in his hands. Mr. Tobias instantly followed.

Josh was confused for a second, but then he saw the bear appear in the doorway. It staggered and fell with a furious roar, but it quickly dragged itself back up on all four feet. It stood weaving drunkenly, bellowing its anger from a mouth full of terrible teeth.

Out of the corner of his eye, Josh saw the copilot sag against one of the floats on the opposite side of the wing. The second float had been broken off and now bobbed like a long cork next to the fuselage, the main body of the airplane.

Tyler cupped his hands to his mouth and yelled to the copilot, "Uncle Ross! Are you all right?"

Mr. Ashby weakly raised his hand and tried to wave reassuringly, but Josh could tell the man was hurt. The pilot also realized that, Josh noticed, for Mr. Dabner moved cautiously along the wing toward his companion.

Tyler broke Josh's concentration, saying, "We've got to get a fire started or we'll all die."

Shivering uncontrollably, Josh looked at the other boy. "You got matches?" he asked.

"No," Tyler replied through chattering teeth, "but some of them will." He motioned toward the plane, where the two pilots on the wing sat down and slid feet first into the icy water. "First law of survival in Alaska," Tyler added, "is get warm and dry. Even a cheechako should know that."

Josh ignored the intended insult. "I know about fire and shelter," he answered. "I'll find something to burn."

"Everything will be wet," Tyler reminded him. "You'll have to dig under fallen logs and against rocks where it might still be dry. We need small stuff, like twigs, for kindling. Then larger branches and other wood."

"I know." Josh started toward a dead snag of tree, but he spun around when he heard yelling from the lake.

The heads of all four men were bobbing in the water. Josh sensed Mr. Blenker and Mr. Tobias's urgency in getting life jackets on the pilot and copilot.

"Look out!" Tyler yelled suddenly. "The bear!"

Josh snapped his gaze away from the men to the cargo door. He was just in time to see the animal clumsily slide out of the aircraft and into the water. Josh's mind screamed, *It's still too drowsy from the drug! It'll drown!*

Tyler broke into Josh's concern for the bear. "You won't

find any wood standing there shivering!" he said.

Josh clenched his teeth to keep them from chattering, but that didn't help. He glanced back at the water. All four men were paddling for shore, buoyed by their orange life jackets. The copilot used only one hand to paddle and seemed to be gasping for each breath. Josh wasn't sure if that was from the extreme cold or his injuries.

Josh looked for the bear, but it had disappeared.

It drowned, Josh thought, feeling sorry for the animal. He turned and started looking for fuel but was soon stopped by the sound of a mighty growl behind him.

Spinning around, Josh saw that the plane had sunk, leaving only a huge air bubble on the lake's surface. But the groggy bear had managed to slide one great forepaw across the float that had broken off when the plane hit the water. It clung there, helplessly roaring in anger at the four men in the water.

A moment before, Josh had felt sorry for the bear, but now he had mixed feelings. He was glad the bear hadn't drowned, yet obviously it wasn't going to be friendly to the people if it got ashore on the same island.

The cold air on Josh's wet clothes promptly reminded him that hypothermia* was closing in on him. He turned away from the bear. "Got to have a fire," he mumbled as he forced his shaking body toward the snag. "I hope there's something dry enough to burn over there."

He found nothing dry or burnable at the snag. Josh stared down in disappointment. *There's got to be something dry around here,* he told himself. *I've got to find it. Maybe under one of those downed logs where the rain doesn't fall.*

He approached two logs that had fallen across each other, but he found that a small rivulet running under them had soaked the twigs. In frustration, he looked around for some other possible source of dry tinder. Moisture dripped from brush and small trees, but there was no sheltered spot under the steady rain.

"Josh!" The pilot's voice cut through the boy's disappointment. He turned toward the other five people who were now standing in a tight circle. "Come over here," Mr. Dabner called. "We've got to check everyone out."

"I've got to find some dry wood," Josh said through chattering teeth.

"We'll all help in a minute, but first let's assess our situation. So come on over so we can check you out."

Josh quickly joined the four men and the boy, who were all shivering as much as he was. The copilot sat on the wet ground, his left arm held protectively over his ribs.

Tyler knelt beside his uncle. No one said anything, but Josh guessed that Mr. Ashby had internal injuries.

The pilot had a gash on his forehead, where a bump was already rising. Mr. Blenker thought he had sprained his right wrist. Mr. Tobias was limping from twisting his knee. Everyone shivered violently in wet clothes.

Mr. Dabner looked at the two boys and asked, "Either of you hurt?"

"I'm okay," Josh replied. He held out his arm with the bandage—now thoroughly soaked. "I got this earlier."

Tyler said, "I'm fine. Couple of bruises is all."

"All right," the pilot said. "Except for Ross, we're in pretty good shape. I suspect he's got a broken rib or two. We need to get a fire going and build a shelter, and then we'll consider our situation further. First, who's got matches?"

"I do," Mr. Tobias replied, reaching into his shirt pocket and producing a soggy paper book of them. "But they're useless."

"I have dry ones," Mr. Blenker said. He held up a small, metal container with his shaking fingers. "Waterproof."

The survivors gave a small cheer as the fish and game officer started to remove the cap.

"Uh oh!" he whispered. He held the container up so that everyone could see water trickle out. "The lid got bent." He quickly removed the cap and poured the wooden matches into his palm. "They're too wet to strike."

The pilot asked quietly, "Anybody have dry ones?"

When there was no answer, Josh saw a look of understanding slowly cross each man's face.

Without matches, there would be no fire. And without fire, all six of them faced death from cold and exposure.

Chapter Six

A DESPERATE NEED

We'll be all right if we use our heads," Mr. Dabner said as firmly as possible through chattering teeth. "The first thing is to take off our wet clothes and wring them out the best we can."

Tyler protested, "What good will that do? It's raining so hard that we'll just get wet all over again."

"The rain isn't nearly as cold as lake water," the pilot replied, unbuttoning his shirt. "As you all know, the first law of Alaskan survival is to stay as warm and dry as possible. Take your clothes off and wring them out. Then we'll have to find some way to start a fire and make a shelter."

Josh had already begun looking without success for something to burn, but he didn't say anything. He removed his shoes and emptied the water that had been squishing inside. He took off his pants, then his shirt, and wrung them out. The cold wind caused goose bumps all over his body. He shook so violently that it was difficult to struggle back into his damp clothes.

Tyler said through chattering teeth, "One good thing about the rain and wind: It keeps the mosquitoes away. But if the wind drops to under five miles an hour, they'll be after us by the millions."

Josh glanced at the sky, which looked as though it might begin to clear before too long. He had already heard about Alaska's maddening hordes of buzzing insects. With no repellent, Josh wondered how they would protect themselves from the swarming little blood-suckers.

His thoughts were interrupted by the pilot. "Your guns are wet," he said to Mr. Blenker, Mr. Ashby, and Mr. Tobias. "But the powder in your cartridges will be dry. We can remove the bullets, pour the powder onto some dry, flammable material, and then fire the gun. The flash from the primer should give us enough flame to start our fire. Meanwhile, let's find out what we have on hand to keep us alive."

Mr. Blenker said, "I tried to grab survival gear from the tail section, but it was jammed in. I couldn't get a thing."

"Then we'll have to make do with what we've got," the pilot replied. He began getting dressed again. "Dig through your pockets, everyone."

All three officers and Tyler had pocket knives, but nobody had a hatchet or other tool. Mr. Blenker had two candy bars, which he offered to share. Mr. Tobias said he would do the same with a pack of gum. There was no food, and berries wouldn't be ripe, but with the officers' heavy-caliber revolvers, they figured they might be able to shoot some small game.

As for drinking water, the pilot said, Alaska's streams and lakes might have giardia* or other harmful micro-organisms. But rainwater was safe to drink. Their immediate needs were for heat, shelter, and medical attention for Tyler's uncle. But they didn't even have a first-aid kit.

Mr. Dabner assured the other survivors, "The average rescue from an Alaskan crash site is just two days. We might get a little hungry, but we won't starve. The Civil Air Patrol, or CAP, will be out looking for us by tomorrow morning. As soon as we get a fire going to keep warm, we'll also build signal fires. We'll probably all be safely home tomorrow."

Trying to hide his nervousness, Josh asked as casually as possible, "Don't we have any other way of signaling rescuers?"

Tyler exclaimed, "Sure!" He turned to the copilot, who was still holding his chest. "Uncle Ross, you told me that planes carry an emergency transmitter. You know, the kind that automatically sends out a signal when a plane crashes?"

"You mean an Emergency Locator Transmitter, or ELTS," the copilot said, wincing in pain.

The pilot explained, "That sank with the plane, and there wasn't a hand-held set on board."

"A little bit of smoke in thousands of acres of trees is going to be hard to spot," Tyler said, still shivering. "The plane sank, so searchers won't be able to find the wreckage, either. Isn't there some other way to help them find us?"

Mr. Dabner spoke calmly but firmly. "We'll do everything possible to take care of ourselves," he said, "and sooner or later, the CAP search teams will find us. Now, there's no use standing here talking. Put your life jackets back on. They'll help keep us warm. Then those of you who are able, spread out and search for something to start a fire. Maybe we can find some rocks that will produce sparks from our knives. We also need to get wood for a shelter."

Mr. Tobias suggested, "Look for a birch tree or a dead cottonwood. They'll give us our best chance of finding dry material to burn. But from here, I see only spruce trees and lots of alders."

"Spread out and get what you can," Mr. Dabner said. "Oh, and look out for that bear in case he got ashore. He may be afraid of us, or he might want revenge for what we did to him.

"One of you had better leave your pistol here, though," he continued. "I'll start removing the bullets to get at the powder."

"Isn't that dangerous?" Tyler asked.

"Not if you know how," Mr. Dabner assured him. "Now let's scatter, but don't lose sight of this spot. We don't want anyone to get lost. While you're scouting for dry fuel, find some downed trees or limbs that will help make a shelter. Those of you with knives can cut some of the higher branches off alder clumps. There are lots of them growing all around. When we get a fire going and a shelter up, we'll take another look at things."

Josh turned to leave, but Tyler stopped him. "Hey, cheechako," he said, "you'd better stick with me if you want to stay alive in this wilderness."

"Mr. Dabner said we're to spread out," Josh replied, starting off again.

"Don't turn your back on me!" Tyler said. He took a

couple of quick steps to catch up. "In a way, it's all your fault we're in this mess!"

"Mine? How do you figure that?"

"You're the one that got those people to relocate that bear." Tyler motioned toward the two rangers and the fish and game officer.

"The bear jumped you first," Josh replied evenly. "Not that it makes any difference. That bear had to be relocated, and you and I just happened to get involved. Now, I've got things to do." He walked away from the other boy.

"Watch out for that bear!" Tyler called. "I hear he especially likes to eat cheechakos."

Glancing at the lake, Josh's eyes strained for any sign of the animal. There was none. Then Josh saw something in the willows by the shore. He took another good look.

The pontoon! he realized. Did the bear get to shore on that, or did the wind make the pontoon drift ashore after the bear fell off?

With some effort, Josh forced his mind off that subject and concentrated on finding flammable material. He reminded himself to ask the pilot more about the Civil Air Patrol when he got back to camp.

It was difficult walking through the alders, which didn't grow like the alders he had seen in California. There they were trees. Here in Alaska they were more like low, tangled clumps of dripping-wet brush.

His thoughts flashed to Tank. *I wish he was here. No, I wouldn't wish this situation on him, but it would sure be better to have him along than Tyler.*

Forcing the thought away, Josh raised his gaze to sweep the area ahead of him. *There!* He looked harder. *Yes!* Beyond a tangle of berry bushes, he saw a small, sheltered spot below a fallen log. Maybe the water hadn't reached there and he could find something dry to start a fire.

Eagerly, Josh hurried forward, but then he stopped abruptly and his heart started racing.

Something was moving in the berry bushes.

* * *

The rain had stopped in Fireweed, and the sun probed bright fingers through the dispersing clouds. Tank stood at his bedroom window, watching the changes. He had lived in Alaska long enough to know that the sun would not set until about 15 minutes before midnight this late in June. That would give Josh plenty of time to leave the relocated bear and return before dark.

In fact, Tank thought, *Josh could be returning to Lake Hood about now.* But somehow, Tank was not reassured. The strange, unexplainable feeling he had experienced earlier still disturbed him.

Sure, he admitted to himself, *I'm upset with him. Why shouldn't I be? But it's really Alicia's fault. I don't know why she keeps butting in where she's not wanted. Well, it's not going to stop until he quits taking her side against me.*

The telephone's ringing momentarily disrupted his thoughts. He heard his mother's voice answering it, but he couldn't make out her words. He stood staring out the window until he heard her call.

"It's for you, Tank," she said.

"Who is it?"

Mrs. Catlett hesitated, then answered evasively, "Why don't you answer it and find out for yourself?"

"Mom! I'm not in the mood for games."

"It's no game. I think you should answer it."

"Oh, all right. It's probably Ryan or Jacob. Maybe Luke or some of the other guys."

Tank didn't feel like talking to them, but he was new in the neighborhood. He would have to start making new friends if he and Josh weren't going to be best friends anymore.

He picked up the receiver. "Yeah? Who is it?" he asked.

"Don't hang up!" The girl's voice sounded a little concerned. "I want to tell you something. It may not mean a thing, but—"

"Who is this?" he interrupted.

"Alicia. Please listen to me!"

Tank started to slam down the receiver, but there was something in her tone that made him pause. "Yeah?"

"It may be nothing," she began, "but . . . well, I thought I should tell you."

Tank's curiosity rose. "Tell me what?"

"My father was down at the CAP a while ago—"

"What's that?" he demanded impatiently.

"It stands for Civil Air Patrol. They're volunteer pilots and observers who help look for . . . well, for planes that are reported missing."

Tank's throat tightened suddenly, as if someone had pulled a noose around it. "Planes missing?" he cried, his voice cracking. "Are you saying . . .?"

"No! No! Daddy was there when he heard a report about a very brief signal from an Emergency Locator Transmitter, or ELTS. That's a battery-operated gadget that's automatically triggered to send out a signal when . . . uh . . . when a plane stops suddenly. Really suddenly."

"You mean a crash?" Tank's voice sounded strange in his ears. "Is that what you mean?"

"Yes, but this particular signal only lasted a few seconds, so maybe some pilot accidentally turned it on."

Tank remembered the strange feeling he'd had earlier. He asked softly, "When did this happen?"

"An hour or so ago. As I said, it's probably nothing, or maybe just a pilot error, but I thought of Josh—"

"Was it Josh's plane?" Tank broke in.

"Nobody knows whose plane it was. When the ELTS works right, it sends out a continuous signal that searchers can follow to the source."

Tank closed his eyes, trying to blot out the possibility that the signal came from Josh's plane.

Alicia asked in his ear, "You still there?"

"Yeah." He took a deep breath and forced himself to pose the question he didn't want to ask. "If it wasn't turned off accidentally, what else could cause the signal to stop?"

There was a long pause before Alicia answered, "It might have sunk somewhere."

"No!" Tank yelled into the mouthpiece. "That didn't happen! You're just saying that to scare me because Josh and I got into an argument!"

"I wouldn't do a terrible thing like—"

"Yes, you would!" Tank was vaguely aware that his mother had come running to stand beside him. She was asking him something, but he couldn't focus on her words.

Tank shouted into the phone, "I don't like you, Alicia! But I would never make up anything as awful as that!"

"I'm sorry, Tank. I shouldn't have called."

The phone clicked dead. Tank removed it from his ear and stared at the receiver.

His mother said sharply, "Answer me! What happened?"

"Nothing, Mom! She just made up a terrible story to make me feel bad! Well, it's not going to work!"

He ran down the hallway to his room, ignoring his mother's frantic calls.

* * *

Josh stood stone still while his eyes tried to make out what was moving in the dense berry bushes. *What will I do if it's the bear?* he wondered.

Suddenly, about 15 feet away, the bushes parted and a catlike creature with tufted ears peered out at him. It was bigger than a bobcat and smaller than a mountain lion, which Josh had seen in zoos.

A lynx! The realization snapped into his memory bank.

Would it attack people? If so, the animal could be upon him in two quick leaps.

Neither boy nor lynx moved a muscle. Their eyes locked and held. The cat's eyes had an almost hypnotic effect. They were wide, unblinking, and cold. Yet they had a strange attractiveness, too. The animal was beautiful in a wild, primitive way.

"Hey, cheechako!" Tyler's voice off to the left made Josh turn his head. "Don't just stand there! Get busy!"

Josh turned back toward the lynx, but it was gone. It hadn't made a sound. Not even a leaf stirred on the bushes where the animal must have disappeared. It was as though Josh had imagined the whole thing.

"Hey!" One of the men yelled off to Josh's right. "I found something that should burn. I've also cut some alders."

"Me, too," another man called.

"Then everybody come on back," the pilot shouted. "Let's get the fire going and start a shelter."

Josh was only too glad to obey. He headed empty-handed toward the camp as Tyler rounded a fallen cottonwood log, dragging a couple of dead limbs.

"You were goofing off out there, cheechako," Tyler said accusingly. "We're all in danger for our lives, and you're standing around daydreaming!"

"I wasn't—"

"Don't lie to me! I saw you. Now, maybe you don't care about your own useless life, but the rest of us care about ours—especially me. So you had better watch your step!"

Chapter Seven

WHEN A PLANE IS MISSING

A few minutes later, back in what Mr. Dabner was calling "our camp," all but one of the shivering survivors huddled close together for warmth. They anxiously watched the pilot as he squatted on the wet ground, trying to start a fire in the light rain.

Directly opposite from him, the copilot, Mr. Ashby, was still hunched over, holding his chest. He hadn't complained, but it was obvious that his broken ribs were causing severe pain.

Tyler didn't seem too concerned, making Josh wonder if the boy didn't realize how much pain his uncle was in or if Tyler simply didn't care.

The pilot spoke, bringing Josh's attention back to him. "Let's hope this works," he said, placing a cartridge into the .357 magnum pistol he had borrowed from the copilot.

He had removed the lead bullet from a cartridge and carefully poured out the powder on top of a small tepee of tinder made of moss, leaves, and pieces of bark laid on a foundation of large tree branches.

"Now," the pilot explained, "only the primer remains in the

shell. When I fire the gun, let's hope the flame that shoots out will be enough to start a blaze in our little pile of tinder."

He aimed the weapon at the tepee, adding, "This isn't as dry as I'd like, but it's all we've got."

Josh instinctively braced himself, anticipating a loud bang as Mr. Dabner pulled the trigger. Flames from the primer shot out of the barrel and ignited the powder. It flashed brightly.

"It's burning!" Tyler cried excitedly.

A small cheer erupted from the other survivors, but that quickly faded to a groan when the powder burned off without catching the moss and other material on fire.

"Too wet," the pilot said in a disappointed tone. "We need drier fuel, but it's not available. Maybe if we empty twice the powder for a second shot . . ." He didn't finish his sentence but began carefully removing the lead from two more cartridges.

Josh glanced back at the injured copilot. Josh felt sure that Mr. Dabner had examined Tyler's uncle while everyone else had been looking for fuel. The pilot hadn't shared his findings with the other four survivors, but the copilot's silent suffering added urgency to the need for fire and shelter.

Everyone huddled close together and silently watched the pilot prepare for a second try at starting a fire.

Josh's heart pounded in concern that there would be another failure. He didn't want to show any signs of fear, though, especially in front of Tyler.

"We're about ready," the pilot announced quietly, again aiming the revolver at the power poured on the moss and leaves.

Josh held his breath.

Flames from the primer again streaked out of the barrel. The powder flashed briefly, but the fuel still didn't catch. A low moan escaped from one of the men.

"Maybe the third time is the charm," the pilot mused, and he carefully removed another bullet from the gun.

Josh noticed that nobody else even looked up. They all kept their eyes averted to avoid eye contact. Josh suspected they were thinking of home, family, and friends, as he was.

I imagine Mom and Dad are worried sick by now, Josh thought. *My big sister and little brother probably are, too. And Tank? I wonder what he's thinking?*

Josh wished he and Tank hadn't parted with bad feelings between them. *I really miss having Tank with me,* Josh thought. *But now I'm glad he's not here in this terrible predicament.*

"Last try," the pilot said, and he fired the pistol a third time. There was a flash, a spark of hope, and then only the rain hissing as it fell on the unlighted fuel.

A collective sigh of disappointment passed through the other survivors, and the pilot turned to face them. "While you were away from camp," he said, "I tried making sparks by striking rocks together, but that didn't work. Neither did striking a knife on metal. So for now, all we can do is build a shelter and hope that tomorrow the sun will shine and we find dry fuel to light a fire."

He paused, looking at each person in turn before continuing. "We must be realistic and practical. It's up to us to find ways to survive until we're rescued. Our top priorities are to remain calm and build a shelter."

Hesitating for a moment, he added quietly, "If any of you knows how to pray, now's a good time to do it."

As the group dispersed, Tyler stepped over to face Josh. "Hey, cheechako," Tyler said, "come with me and I'll show you how to find things we can use."

Josh looked the other boy squarely in the eye. "Relax, Tyler, you don't have to prove anything to me," he said.

Tyler's face darkened. "I was just trying to help you," he insisted.

Josh didn't believe that. "I think I'll go with Mr. Tobias," he said. Josh quickly turned to the ranger and asked, "Is that okay with you?"

"Sure," Mr. Tobias answered, adjusting the pistol in the holster at his belt. "I could use your help."

Josh stepped around the other boy to join Mr. Tobias. "Thanks," he said. "And thanks for looking after me in the plane after we hit the water."

"You're welcome. Let's try inland, away from the lake shore."

Josh followed the man as he pressed through waist-high brush. The light branches easily gave way, then sprang back, spraying cold water into Josh's face.

"How badly hurt is the copilot?" Josh asked.

"We think he broke a rib or two, but his lungs weren't punctured or the symptoms would be different. He said it hurts to breathe, so he's taking shallow breaths. That could lead to pneumonia. But he'll be okay if the CAP finds us soon."

"How do they search for people?"

"The Civil Air Patrol is pretty well organized, although it's made up entirely of unpaid volunteers. The CAP is an auxiliary of the U. S. Air Force and operates under their guidance and control. When Alaska state troopers report a plane is missing, they notify the Rescue Coordinator Center, or RCC. They're headquartered at Elmendorf Air Force Base in Anchorage. RCC gets CAP involved by opening a mission and assigning a mission number to it. Then the search begins."

"How do they do that?" Josh asked.

Mr. Tobias explained, "The CAP's Polaris Squadron is located at Merrill Field in Anchorage. On the wall they have a huge map of Alaska. The entire state is broken up into grids, or squares. Each has a latitude and longitude designation, and each grid has a number assigned to it. Each grid can be broken down further into quarters: Alpha, Bravo, Charley, and Delta sections of the grid.

"The top left is Alpha, next to it on the right is Bravo, lower left is Charley, and lower right is Delta. In Alaska, these grids cover mountains, rivers, and just about every other kind of terrain."

Josh tried hard to understand, because his life and the lives of the other survivors depended on those volunteers from the Civil Air Patrol.

"RCC assigns each participating plane to a particular grid

or section of a grid," the ranger continued. "There are some 1,140 grids of about 30 miles by 30 miles each. Each grid can be broken down into those four sections of 15 by 15 miles, and into even smaller segments for searching. Depending on the terrain, the planes fly parallel tracks, if possible, at approximately 800 feet above the ground and at a reasonably slow speed. They try to stay under 100 mph. They fly routes approximately a mile and a quarter apart. A pilot may search a section spanning about seven miles by seven miles over three or four hours."

"So planes fly over these squares looking for a missing plane?" Josh asked.

"Yes. Searching each grid from the air takes several hours. Only a couple of planes are allowed in an area during a search. No other civilian airplanes are allowed in there. There's a pilot in each aircraft, of course, and at least one observer. The pilot has to keep the RCC notified of how much gas he has left and that sort of thing."

"What happens when the CAP finds the missing plane?"

"It depends. Sometimes a search plane can land and pick up survivors, but other times the air force uses a helicopter to rescue survivors."

Josh couldn't help sounding anxious when he asked, "You think they'll find us?"

"It's just a matter of time."

Josh wondered if it would be *in* time.

Mr. Tobias hesitated, then asked, "Josh, how long have you lived in Alaska?"

"About a month."

"That why the other kid is picking on you?"

"I guess so. I sure didn't do anything to him. But he was born here and knows a lot about Alaska. He figures I don't know anything."

"You open to learning some tips about Alaska?"

"I'd like that a lot." Josh trailed his guide through the brush while the ground beneath alternated between long, tough strands of grass and slippery, muddy spots. Josh seemed to be either tripping or sliding, trying to keep his balance in boots that squished with water that had seeped back inside.

Mr. Tobias came to a small clearing and stopped to look around. "As you know, most of Alaska is true wilderness, with all kinds of dangers," he said. "Yet all around us are natural items we can use to help survive those dangers."

He paused, his gaze skimming ahead and from side to side. "As for starting a fire, there should be some birch trees around. Peeling off all the bark will kill the tree, but we need only a small amount. Birches have layer after layer of bark, thin as paper, which you can peel back with your fingers and shred like paper. Josh, do you know how to recognize a birch tree?"

"I think so, but I don't see any around here."

"You're right. This is mostly black spruce, but over there is a dead cottonwood tree. They make good fire starter, too, especially if the inside has dry-rot. That wood can be rubbed to powder and used as tinder tomorrow to start a fire, if the sun comes out."

"You mean with a magnifying glass?" Josh asked.

"I doubt we have one, but we do have watch crystals. Same principle, as I'll show you if the rain stops."

The ranger again shoved his way through the brush, with Josh close behind. "On the ground to your right," Mr. Tobias said, "there are some dead spruce limbs we can use for either shelter or fuel. We'll get those on our way back to camp."

He walked a few more steps before speaking again. "You thinking about your home and family?" he asked.

A pang of loneliness made Josh hesitate before answering, especially when he thought of his parents and of Tank. "Yes," Josh answered quietly. "A lot."

"Me, too. Wife and two daughters. But don't worry. We'll soon be home safe and sound."

"Including the copilot?"

"I hope so." The man started walking again. "But it would sure help to get him out of here and to a doctor."

"Maybe they'll find us tomorrow—" Josh interrupted himself and stopped. "Listen! What's that?"

Mr. Tobias halted and was silent for several seconds. "I don't hear anything," he said quietly.

Listening a moment longer, Josh shrugged. "I don't either. Probably my imagination."

The ranger nodded and circled an alder clump. "The bottom limbs on these alders are too thick to cut without a hatchet. But on the way back from that cottonwood, we'll use my knife to gather some of the branches from higher up, then—"

He halted, interrupted by the sound of something crashing through the trees and brush.

"The bear!" Josh exclaimed, freezing in place.

The animal suddenly burst through the tall brush, charging toward the two people!

* * *

Tank left his bedroom and approached his mother in the kitchen. "Were you just on the phone?" he asked.

"I called Mary Ladd to ask if Josh was home yet."

Tank hesitated before asking, "Is he?"

"No, not yet."

"It's past time he was back."

"I know. So does his mother."

"Do you have Alicia's phone number?"

"Yes." She looked thoughtfully at him. "I didn't think you wanted to talk to her."

"I don't, but I have to find out if there's been anything else from that emergency signal she mentioned."

Mrs. Catlett opened the top drawer beneath the wall phone. "The number is right here."

"Uh . . . would you call her?"

"I think you should do that yourself."

"Aw, Mom! She'll just make me angry again!"

"Anger is something we can control." She lifted the phone and handed it to Tank. "Try it."

Without enthusiasm, he dialed.

Alicia answered on the first ring, suggesting to Tank that she had been waiting by the phone.

"This is Tank," he said stiffly. "You heard any more about that airplane signal?"

"No." The single word held such a note of sadness that Tank flinched. "But Daddy talked to someone at the airport. Josh's plane is overdue," she added.

Tank licked his suddenly dry lips. "What . . . what does that mean?"

"It means that something happened to the plane. Daddy says it must have happened real fast, because there was no radio call."

A monstrous wave of mixed sorrow, pain, and regret crashed over Tank like a December wave off Hawaii's north shore. He had to wait a couple of seconds before he could speak again. "Maybe their plane's radio was broken."

"Maybe." Alicia's tone indicated she didn't really believe that. She added quietly, "Daddy says that if the plane had enough altitude, the pilot almost surely would have sent out a distress radio call."

"Like May Day calls I've seen in movies?"

"Yes, but up here in Alaska the usual procedure is more casual. Most of the time, they just identify the plane by number, then give the location and the nature of the emergency. That way, searchers have some idea of what happened and where to look if the plane goes down."

Tank had to force his next question. "There was none of that?"

"Nothing."

Lowering the phone, Tank closed his eyes and leaned his forehead against the kitchen wall. He vainly tried to shake off a terrible mental picture of Josh's plane unexpectedly plunging into the high mountains.

His mother cried, "What is it?"

With an effort, Tank opened his eyes, blinked back hot tears, and repeated what Alicia had said.

Before he had finished, his mother declared, "I'm going over to be with Josh's mother."

She hurried toward the door while Alicia's voice came over the receiver. Tank slowly lifted it to his ear. "I'm sorry," Tank said into the phone. "What did you just say?"

"I said that Daddy just learned the state police have been notified that Josh's plane is missing. In Alaska, most emergencies start with the state troopers. They call others to help if it's necessary. This time of year, it'll be daylight until nearly midnight, so maybe they'll start a search tonight."

Tank grasped at this straw of hope. "Where would they look?"

"Pilots file a flight plan before every trip. That tells when and where they're going and when they expect to reach their destination or be back."

Tank asked eagerly, "Then there's a chance Josh and the others might be found tonight?"

"It's possible, but we shouldn't get our hopes up. Alaska is a huge state. Most of it's mountain wilderness. Even knowing the general direction of where to search, it takes time."

Tank's spirits sagged. "So they're probably not going to be found tonight?"

"Not likely, but Daddy is a member of the CAP, and he plans to join the search if one is called for tomorrow. I'll go along as an observer."

"Take me with you!" The words spurted out.

After a moment's hesitation, Alicia explained, "Adults are usually the observers. They're trained to know how to spot wreckage—"

"Don't say that!" Tank interrupted. He shook his head to clear away an image of Josh's plane smashed against a mountainside.

"I'm sorry, Alicia," he added quickly and contritely. "I'm just very worried."

"Me, too." Her voice was soft, almost a whisper.

"Josh and I have been through lots of dangerous experiences, but we've always been together. I've flown a lot. I could be a good observer."

"I understand how you feel, but—"

Tank broke in, trying to sound logical and yet make his point. "If I can't be with him wherever he is, the least I can do is try to help find him. I'll do whatever it takes to do that, so please ask your dad!"

For several seconds, the girl didn't reply. Then she said, "I'll talk to him."

"Call me back as soon as you can—please."

"I will."

Tank replaced the phone and turned to look out the

window. The rain had stopped there in Fireweed, and the sun was shining. Everything looked beautiful and peaceful, but Tank's insides churned with remorse. He remembered how he and Josh had parted in anger. A horrible realization smashed into Tank with the force of a blow. A low groan escaped him.

Maybe I'll never see Josh again.

Chapter Eight

THE SEARCH BEGINS

Look out!" Josh yelled as the bear burst from the undergrowth and charged with a furious bellow.

Josh instinctively took a step back, but his foot slipped on the muddy ground. He fell backward, vainly grabbing for brush to break his fall. He glimpsed Mr. Tobias drawing his heavy revolver, but then the brush blocked Josh's view. He landed on his back in the mud.

The report of the ranger's pistol was so loud that Josh's ears rang painfully. He scrambled to his knees. Mr. Tobias still gripped his revolver, but the bear was out of sight, loudly crashing through the brush.

"Are you okay?" Josh asked anxiously.

"Yes," Mr. Tobias replied, returning the weapon to its holster. "How about you?"

"I'm fine. Did . . . did you shoot it?"

"No. I didn't try. I figured there was time to fire one shot in hope the noise would scare it off. But if it had kept coming . . ." Mr. Tobias shrugged.

Josh and the ranger fell silent, listening to the sounds of the bear's wild flight fading away in the underbrush.

"I'm glad you didn't have to shoot it," Josh said.

"Me, too. But for a moment there, I was afraid it was the bear's life or ours. It was really mad and coming hard. I can't blame it. After all, it was just defending itself from people who had immobilized it with a big needle and flown it in an airplane that bumped around in a storm before crashing into a lake. Then it nearly drowned while still groggy from the drug.

"After we crashed, I saw it trying to climb onto that pontoon that broke off the plane. I understand why it doesn't like us, but I'm glad it didn't drown.

"Anyway," Mr. Tobias said, "it's over for now. The sound of my shot will probably bring some of the others running to check on us. But let's not waste time waiting. I want to show you some fire starter that should be in the heart of that dead cottonwood."

Josh followed, asking, "What did you mean about it's over for now?"

"Well, we're all stuck here on this island, which can't be too big. Sooner or later, one of us will stumble on that animal again."

"Somebody like me or Tyler who doesn't have a gun?"

"Yes, or one of the men. There are four of us and only three guns."

Josh asked thoughtfully, "What can we do?"

"Just be careful, and hope we can get off this island before we have to shoot the bear or it seriously mauls someone. Now, here's our tree. Let me show you what we're looking for."

* * *

Tank waited by the phone so that when it rang, he snatched it up on the first ring. "Hello?" he said.

"It's Alicia." For once, her voice was welcome in his ear.

"Yes. What did you find out?"

"Daddy says he doesn't want any tension in the plane while he's flying on a search mission."

"Tension?" Tank repeated.

"Between you and me."

"Oh."

"He wants promises from both of us that if he lets you come along tomorrow, we won't take verbal potshots at each other but will concentrate on helping find Josh's plane."

"I promise," Tank eagerly answered.

"Are you sure?"

"I'm sure!" His voice started to rise. "I'm sure," he repeated more calmly.

"You sound angry."

"I'm not! I'm just—" Tank checked himself. "I'm not angry, at least, not anymore." He added quietly, "I'm just anxious to fly tomorrow and help find Josh. Now, I promised. Tell your dad. All right?"

"I'll tell him."

"Thanks. What time shall I meet you? And where?"

"Can you get a ride to Merrill Field in Anchorage?"

"I'll be there, even if I have to walk."

"Just a minute." Alicia's voice became muffled, indicating

to Tank that she had covered the mouthpiece to speak to her father.

"All right," she said into the phone a few seconds later. "Eight o'clock, if the weather is good. If it isn't, I'll call you and let you know if the search has been postponed."

"Thanks, Alicia," Tank said, before replacing the phone.

His thoughts leaped across the miles to wherever Josh was—and to what shape he might be in.

Only when Tank started to dial the Ladds' house to tell them the plan did he stop and frown. The thought occurred to him, *I promised. But did Alicia? If she didn't, being in that little plane with her tomorrow could be a big problem.*

* * *

Josh and Mr. Tobias approached the standing dead cottonwood. Josh glanced around nervously. He wondered, *Where is that bear? Could Tyler run into it? Or is the bear hiding someplace ahead of Mr. Tobias and me, waiting to attack?*

Josh forced his thoughts off the bear and turned to watch the park ranger.

"Look," Mr. Tobias said, extending his open palm toward Josh to show dry, rotted wood from inside the dead tree trunk. "The wood was protected from the rain and wind. It's not only dry, but it will also crumble into a powder to burn easily. Grab a handful, along with some dry leaves."

As Josh began collecting the tinder, Mr. Tobias said with satisfaction, "On the way back to camp, I'll show you some spruce trees with small, dead twigs that are full of resin that will help to ignite the flames. Our hands are full right now, so we'll have to come back to break off those twigs. With them and our dry wood, we can have a fire tomorrow if the sun comes out."

Following the shoreline back to camp, Josh tripped over something half-buried in the brush. Using his foot, he uncovered the object. "What's this?" he asked.

Mr. Tobias glanced at the long paddle with blades on both ends. "It's used by kayakers so they don't have to keep switching sides when paddling," he said.

Josh exclaimed hopefully, "It's in pretty good shape, so somebody must have lost it fairly recently."

"Maybe someone does live close by on the mainland," Mr. Tobias acknowledged. He glanced across the open expanse of lake between the island and the tree-lined main shore. Then he sighed and said, "But a paddle is useless without a kayak* or canoe in which to cross over."

"I know, but maybe I could use it as a club in case that bear shows up again."

"I wouldn't count on it. A kayak paddle is pretty awkward, and it's not strong enough to stop a mad bear anyway."

"Just the same," Josh answered, "I'd feel better with it in my hands. If I can get it under my arm . . ."

It took him a while, but with hands full of dry cottonwood heart, he used his foot to tip up one end of the paddle. Then he went down on his knees and used his closed fists to slide the handle up under his left armpit. When both ends of the paddle were balanced, he clamped his arm down tightly, holding the long paddle against his rib cage.

"There," he said with satisfaction as he got to his feet. "It's not as good as your gun, but it's better than nothing."

Mr. Tobias and Josh started back toward camp, but Josh stopped almost immediately. He sniffed the air. "Do you smell smoke?" he asked.

Mr. Tobias tested the air. "I don't smell anything," he said.

Sighing, Josh admitted, "Maybe it's just wishful thinking."

He followed the ranger back to camp. There, Josh dropped the paddle and saw that the pilot had driven two forked sticks into the ground about 10 feet apart. He had slanted them so their notched ends touched at the top. A longer limb had been used as a ridgepole. Its top end rested in the notch of the two upright poles, while the other end was imbedded in the soft ground.

Under the guidance of the experienced rangers and fish and game officer, spruce and alder branches were laid across the three original poles. In a short time, a rude shelter began to take shape. When the sides and roof were in place, the survivors pulled some of the coarse, wild grass with thick stems, along with other grass that was almost as fine as hair. These were woven between the branches.

The result was a shelter so snug that it was nearly dark inside. For the first time since the crash, everyone was out of the rain and wind. But they were all still cold.

Tyler's uncle, the copilot, winced from the pain of each breath. It was an effort to talk, so he remained silent. Everyone sat close together to share their body heat. They talked of food they didn't have, how to keep warm, what they could do to get rescued, and when that might happen.

Mr. Tobias asked the pilot, "I know that you were trying to fly around the storm, so the plane had to be off your flight plan. But do you have any idea how far off, and where we are?"

Josh noticed that the pilot shifted uncomfortably before answering. "I have a pretty good idea," he said. "I've flown over this place a couple of times before."

He didn't explain, so Tyler asked, "Where are we?"

The pilot exchanged glances with the other men. Josh had a feeling they had already discussed this and were as reluctant as the pilot to say anything in front of the boys.

"Well?" Tyler asked sharply.

The pilot said quietly, "While we were still over the mainland, heading for the lake where I could land, I saw three islands. The one we're on is the biggest and closest to the mainland."

Tyler frowned. "So?"

"So," Mr. Dabner added, "I recognized this place. It's called Terror Island."

Josh blurted in surprise, "Terror Island? Why?"

For the first time, Tyler's uncle spoke, with obvious difficulty. "You don't need to know that," he said.

"Yes, I do!" Tyler insisted. "How did it get that name?"

Again, the pilot sought the eyes of the other men. As each slowly nodded, the pilot explained. "A few winters ago, another plane went down here, right on this island." Dropping his voice to almost a whisper, he concluded, "Because of heavy weather, it took the searchers several days before they found the place."

Tyler asked, "Were the people okay?"

"No." The pilot paused, then added, "There was evidence that they all lived a few days, but none were alive when found."

"What happened?" Josh wanted to know.

The pilot sighed. "Probably died of hypothermia."

"That's not going to happen to us!" Tyler cried. He hesitated, then asked fearfully, "Is it?"

"Not if we can help it," the pilot assured him. "But we've got to do whatever we can to get help fast." He glanced at the copilot, whose eyes were closed and whose breathing was labored.

Mr. Blenker, the fish and game officer, added so softly that Josh barely heard the words, "Real fast."

Everyone fell silent, and Josh closed his eyes and said a fervent, silent prayer. When he looked up again, he saw that Mr. Tobias's and Mr. Blenker's heads were bowed. He wondered if they were also praying.

Josh felt a flush of warm hope sweep over his body. He closed his eyes again. "Lord," he prayed, "help me to do something tomorrow that will save us all—before it's too late."

* * *

Tank had not yet adjusted to the fact that it doesn't really get dark in south-central Alaska during June. He had been told that it would be August before darkness and night came together. Now, even in the post-midnight hours, the sky looked more like twilight in Hawaii or California. That made it hard for Tank to sleep, especially when he was so restless.

He realized one good thing about the light, though. When the clock showed 5:00 A.M., he could see that the sky was clear.

"Great weather!" he exclaimed, rolling out of bed. "The search is on!" Even though his parents and sister were still asleep and the house was still, Tank pulled off his pajamas and leaped into the shower.

Today, he thought, *we're going to find Josh, and nothing Alicia can say or do is going to upset me.*

There were clouds on the horizon, but the sun had climbed well into a blue sky when Tank's father dropped him off at Merrill Field in Anchorage. Tank sat impatiently through a briefing at the Civil Air Patrol, where assignments were given for the day's search. Mr. Wharton was given grid 136-8 Bravo.

Tank studied the huge wall map and realized that area covered steep mountains and several lakes. He was disappointed that the Wharton plane had been assigned an area slightly to the left of the path indicated in the flight plan for Josh's plane. To Tank, that meant there was less likelihood that they would find the missing aircraft.

However, he had been told it was possible that yesterday's storm had forced Josh's plane off course. It could be down somewhere in the area where Mr. Wharton was headed.

Alaska's microclimates made it possible for rain to be falling there even though it was clear in Anchorage.

A short time later, Tank was sitting beside Alicia in Mr. Wharton's light, single-engine airplane. It sped down the runway and lifted off from one of the nation's busiest small airports.

From the pilot's seat, Mr. Wharton pushed one side of his headset so his ear was uncovered. He raised his voice to be heard above the noise of the engine. "How are you two doing back there?" he asked.

Tank had been looking out the window on the left side as the aircraft climbed above the city. It spread out on a broad plain, with the Chugach Mountains rising between Anchorage and Tank's home in Fireweed.

"Fine," Tank replied as the sun glinted on Cook Inlet* below. "Just fine."

"Same here, Daddy," Alicia said.

Mr. Wharton glanced over his shoulder at Tank. "Do you understand now what the Civil Air Patrol is and how it functions?"

"Yes, I think so," Tank responded. "I listened carefully to what was said in that room before we took off." He wondered if Josh knew about the CAP. If he did, he might have hope.

Tank recalled television news footage of what previous plane wreckage had looked like from the air. He squeezed his eyelids tightly together, trying to blot out the image of Josh's plane lying in a pile of debris.

He opened his eyes on hearing Alicia's voice. "What's the matter, Tank?" she asked.

"Oh, nothing much," he replied evasively.

"Try to think good thoughts," she replied, reaching out and gently touching his arm.

Surprised at the friendly gesture, he managed a smile. "I will. I'm going to think of Josh being home safe again, and us having a great adventure together."

She returned the smile. "That's the spirit."

Tank nodded and turned again to look out the window. Somewhere ahead and below in the trackless mountain wilderness, Tank realized, Josh was probably having an adventure without him—if he was still alive.

* * *

The strange twilight type of night had kept Josh awake, too. Periodic low moans from the badly injured copilot had contributed to Josh's insomnia. However, the time had not been entirely wasted, for Josh had thought a lot and prayed even more.

Doing that had taken his mind off his empty stomach and the damp, cold clothes that clung to his body. The result was that when the others awoke, Josh had decided on a plan—one that required Tyler's help to carry it out.

Josh crawled out of the shelter behind the other boy and looked toward the horizon. A light wind blew through skies that hadn't cleared after all, and the rain continued.

"Tyler," Josh began, "let's talk."

The other boy eyed Josh suspiciously. "What about?" he asked.

"If we don't work together, we could all be dead before search planes find us."

"You work with some of the men. I don't need you."

Josh ignored the rebuff. "I think you do, and I know I need you. We've already determined that it's too early in the season for berries to be ripe, and not one of us reported seeing anything else to eat."

Josh didn't mention the lynx, which wasn't something he thought of as edible, even if the animal could have been taken. "So," Josh concluded, "if we don't want to end up like those people whose experience caused this place to be called Terror Island, we've got to get over there to the mainland."

Tyler laughed derisively. "You're not only a cheechako, but you're a crazy one at that." He pointed to the lake shore and the densely forested mainland beyond. "That water's so cold that you'd die before very long, even if you could swim that far."

"We won't swim," Josh replied confidentially, "and we'll make it to the other shore and see if we can find someone to help us. I'm pretty sure I smelled smoke yesterday, which had to have come from the mainland. Maybe there's someone living just across the lake in those trees. Even if there isn't, we might find some game—"

"*We?*" Tyler interrupted, his eyes widening in disbelief. "What do you mean, 'we'?"

"You and me." Josh motioned to Tyler and then himself. "Together, we can do it."

Slowly shaking his head, Tyler asked, "Even if I went

along with you on this harebrained idea, how do you plan for us to get over there?"

"I found a kayak paddle yesterday. It's over there by that cottonwood stump. We can use it to—"

Tyler interrupted with a scornful snort. "You're dumber than I thought!" he said. "What good is a paddle if we don't have anything to paddle in?"

Unruffled by the other boy's attitude, Josh said, "Maybe not *in,* but *on.* I'll show you."

Chapter Nine

AN IDEA LEADS TO DANGER

In his eagerness to show Tyler what he had in mind, Josh temporarily forgot the cold and his damp clothes. He first retrieved the kayak paddle he had found and showed it to Tyler, who wasn't impressed.

Undeterred, Josh then led the other boy past a small cottonwood tree with leaves rustling in the slight wind. He pushed through willows lining the lake shore and stopped near where their plane sank.

"I thought about it all night," Josh said over his shoulder, "and I'm pretty sure that yesterday I smelled wood smoke on the mainland." He pointed across the lake. "The source should be right over there in those trees."

"Even if there was smoke," Tyler said scornfully, "there's no way we could get across that cold water."

"I'm not so sure about that." Josh began pushing brush aside and peering through it.

"What're you doing?" Tyler demanded, easing a willow branch out of his way to stand beside Josh.

"I'm looking for the pontoon that broke off when we hit

the water." Josh used the paddle to make a path through the willows until he stood within inches of the lake. His eyes vainly searched the shoreline. "I remember seeing the bear clinging to it in the water."

"So what? The wind could have carried it halfway around the island by now."

"My guess is the bear got ashore on that pontoon. If we can find it, then you and I could use this paddle to cross the lake to the mainland. Somebody must live there."

"We could do *what?*" Tyler cried.

Josh didn't answer but glanced at the tree tops. "The wind is blowing over here from the mainland, so the pontoon probably was blown farther back up along the beach. Help me find it."

"You find it, cheechako. I'm going back to—"

A low "whoof" sound interrupted him.

Both boys whirled around, their eyes skimming past the willows that lined the shore, beyond the cottonwood, to the spruce and alders growing inland.

After a long moment when there was no further sound except for the rustling cottonwood leaves, Tyler whispered, "You think it was that bear?"

"I'm pretty sure of it." Josh kept his voice down while he looked for the bear and gripped the long-handled kayak paddle. It didn't seem like much of a weapon, but it felt better than having empty hands.

Tyler urged, "Let's get back to camp, fast!"

"Wait!" Josh hissed. "It's between us and there."

"But we can't just stay here!"

"No, but we'd better know for sure where it is before we move. We don't want to stumble into it."

Tyler exclaimed in a hoarse, frightened whisper, "He could be sneaking up on us right now!"

"Maybe." Josh glanced up and down the lake shore, his heart pounding. "We might be able to follow the shoreline a while and skirt around the bear to get back to camp."

"Anything's better than standing here!"

Nodding, Josh tried again to spot the bear. "He sounded as if he's over to the left a little, so let's try going to our right. Quietly!"

Wordlessly, Tyler nodded and followed Josh as he slipped as silently as a shadow to the right, carefully pushing lithe willow branches out of his way. Josh moved cautiously, although he wanted to run, getting as far from the angry black bear as possible. There was no further sound from the animal, making Josh wonder if it was silently stalking them. All he heard were some ravens calling and a robin singing somewhere inland.

Suddenly, Josh stopped and listened intently.

Tyler leaned close to whisper in Josh's ear, "What do you hear?"

"I don't know. It's sort of strange."

"The bear?"

"I don't think so, but I can't place it. Come on. Let's find out." Josh slipped forward through the willows with the paddle in front of him. He thought he heard Tyler whimper behind him, but he didn't turn around.

* * *

The light plane had carried Tank, Alicia, and her father out of sunshine and into a light rain over high mountains. Snow still clung to their peaks, ridges, and crevices. Tank scowled as the raindrops splattered against his side window, partially obscuring his vision.

He stirred uneasily when Mr. Wharton twisted in the pilot's seat to glance over his shoulder. Tank silently groaned as he thought, *Oh, no! He's going to tell us we have to turn back because of the weather!*

Mr. Wharton raised his voice to be heard over the steady drone of the single engine. "We've reached our assigned grid," he said. "It's going to be harder to see now, but unless this rain gets worse, we're going to make our first pass anyway. So keep a sharp lookout below."

Heaving a big sigh of relief, Tank smiled gratefully at the pilot, then glanced at Alicia sitting across from him on the right side of the aircraft. "We'll find them," he assured her.

"Either we will or one of the other search planes," she replied, then added, "unless this rain gets worse and we have to turn back."

"That can't happen!" he exclaimed.

"I hope you're right." She resumed looking out her window.

The little plane gave a slight lurch, making Tank uneasy. "Please, God," he whispered, looking through the rain-streaked window. "Please let us find Josh and the others soon. I couldn't live with myself if anything happened and I never got to tell him I'm sorry."

Tank didn't finish his silent prayer because the plane dipped sharply. A frightening thought flashed through his mind: *What would happen if we went down, too?*

* * *

Every bit of Josh's mind and body was keenly alert as he slowly led Tyler toward the strange sound along the lake shore. Soon, Tyler whispered, "See anything?"

"Not yet." Josh kept his tone low. "But we're getting close." He stopped and looked back in the direction from which they had come. "No sign of that bear the last several minutes."

"We must have come halfway around the island."

"Seems like it, but we've been moving slowly and quietly, so it's probably not as far as it seems."

A few more cautious steps through the willows brought Josh to an opening with a beach not more than 15 feet long. "There!" he exclaimed aloud, pointing with the paddle.

"The pontoon!" Tyler exclaimed. The front part rested on the six-foot-wide beach. The rear was repeatedly being lifted by small waves and gently shoved a bit farther onto shore. "That funny noise was the water hitting the back end," he added.

Josh turned to grin at the other boy. "You're right," he said. "Let's take a look at it."

Tyler twisted to look back the way they had come. "You think we're safe now?" he asked.

"I can't see through that brush any better than you, but I think we've lost that ol' bear. Besides, if he comes charging out at us now, we can shove this float into the water, jump on it, and paddle off."

"You cheechakos never learn!" Tyler said. "Bears can swim *real* well! And their bodies are so well insulated that icy cold water doesn't bother them."

Josh was so relieved at finding the pontoon that he managed a relaxed smile as he replied, "We've got a better chance of getting away by skimming over the water than he does swimming with only his head above the surface."

"I suppose so," Tyler admitted, and he followed Josh to inspect the pontoon.

It was in pretty good condition, the boys decided. It had been snapped cleanly from the underside of the wing. There were some dents and scratches, but it was still watertight.

"It held the weight of our plane," Josh said, touching the pontoon with the kayak paddle, "so it will easily hold us."

"Not me!" Tyler shook his head emphatically. "I'm not riding that thing across the lake! I'm going back to camp. Maybe one of the men will risk going with you."

Josh started to protest, but he changed his mind as he looked across the water. "Look!" he said. "See above the tree tops?"

"Smoke! That's smoke! Somebody's over there!"

"Right! Maybe a village way back in the Bush.* We can

paddle across, tell them what happened, and maybe get some help for your uncle! At least we can get a fire going to keep warm, and maybe whoever lives over there can get help fast."

For the first time, Josh noticed that Tyler seemed concerned about his uncle. "Well," Tyler said uncertainly, "I suppose it would be good for Uncle Ross, but I'd rather go back to camp and talk to the men."

"Me, too, but—" An angry roar interrupted Josh. "The bear!" He couldn't see the animal, but he could hear it smashing through underbrush toward the shore. "Quick! Help me shove this float into the water!"

With some frantic pushing, the boys got the pontoon off the beach. They leaped aboard. Josh began trying to paddle, but he wasn't used to having blades on both ends. The pontoon swung around in a circle.

"You're heading toward shore!" Tyler yelled as the bear charged into sight from the willows. "Here! Give me that thing!"

Wordlessly, Josh extended the long paddle to the other boy. He gripped it expertly with both hands well apart and about a foot above each blade. In a few quick strokes, he turned the pontoon around and moved them frantically away from the shore.

Josh swiveled his head to watch the bear race onto the small beach. "Faster, Tyler!" he yelled. "He's still coming!"

"I'm doing the best I can!"

Josh watched the bear hit the water with a mighty splash. It made a couple of strokes with hairy forepaws, then stopped and returned to the beach.

"It's okay!" Josh called. "He's crawling out of the water."

Tyler rested the center of the long handle across his legs and looked back. "Whew! That was scary!" he admitted.

"My heart's trying to break a hole in my ribs," Josh said with a weak smile. "Boy! He would have caught us if we'd stayed on land." Pausing, Josh added thoughtfully, "Or if you hadn't been so good with that paddle."

"I've done my share of kayaking," Tyler replied while the bear stalked along the shore, knocking down willows with angry swipes of his great forepaws.

"I'm glad of that," Josh said. "Real glad."

The boys fell silent, watching the bear.

Josh finally spoke again. "I guess he's going to stay mad. At least, he's not going to let us land around here."

"We could paddle along the shore until we can call to the men in camp to bring a gun," Tyler said.

"Yes." Josh looked back the way they had come, and then across the lake. "But notice that this is the narrowest stretch of water between here and the mainland. We're already pretty far out. We could go on across and try to follow that smoke to its source. Whoever it is will help us."

"Well, we definitely can't go back past that bear," Tyler said as he lifted the paddle again. "You ready?"

"Yes, but do you want me to paddle a while?"

"What? And end up right back by that bear?" Tyler shook his head. "No, thanks! I'll paddle."

As the blades dipped into the water, first on one side of the pontoon and then on the other, Tyler spoke again. "I just had a horrible thought," he said.

"What's that?"

"What if it's not a village over there?"

"It's got to be."

"Not necessarily. If it's a village, there should be lots of smoke. We saw only one column rising above the treetops, so it must come from a cabin."

"It doesn't matter whether it's one person or a place full of people. We need any help we can get."

"If it's only one person, Josh, ask yourself why anybody would live way out here, all alone, in the middle of millions of acres of forest and mountains."

"My dad says Alaska is full of people who want to be by themselves. They like it that way."

"Did he also tell you that sometimes those men don't take kindly to strangers?"

"You mean someone like a hermit?"

"Yes, or maybe a criminal hiding out from the law. A person like that could be real mean."

"I hadn't thought of that," Josh admitted, "but I believe anyone would try to help plane crash survivors. Besides, I think we're just scaring ourselves by talking this way."

"I guess we'll soon find out," Tyler replied, steering the pontoon toward a small clearing free of willows. "Hang on. We're going ashore."

The boys beached their makeshift craft so the wind wouldn't blow it into the lake and strand them. They left the paddle and carefully sniffed the air. The smell of wood smoke was now strong, although it wasn't visible in the light rain.

"That way," Josh decided, pointing to the right and inland.

"I just hope there are no bears over here," Tyler said softly, falling into step beside Josh and heading toward a stand of spruce trees. "Especially grizzlies. Remember the pilot said he saw one on the beach when we flew over it just before the crash?"

"Let's make lots of noise," Josh answered, remembering what he had already learned in Alaska. "That ought to keep them away if there are any around here."

The boys started clapping their hands and chanting, "Hey, bear! Hey, bear!"

They picked their way past alder clumps, stopping occasionally to test the air. They agreed the smell of wood smoke was definitely getting stronger.

"But," Tyler cautioned, "there's no way it can be coming from a village. No dogs are barking. There's no sound of kids playing or people chopping wood. Nothing."

Josh slowed his pace. "Are you trying to scare me?" he asked.

"No, but I think whoever's making that smoke is all by himself, and he may not want company."

"It doesn't matter. When we tell him about the crash, and that we need help, it'll be okay."

"Listen!" Tyler held up his hand.

"What?"

"Shh! Don't you hear it?"

Josh tilted his head. "Yes! I think it's a plane!"

"Coming this way!"

Josh's hopes soared while he glanced up through the trees that surrounded them. "We've got to find an open space so we can signal them! Try to make them see us! This way!"

The boys broke into a mad run toward a clearing.

Suddenly, a tall man with a bushy beard and uncombed hair leaped from behind a tree with an ax handle in hand. "Try to take my gold, will you?" he shouted, rushing toward them. "I'll show you what I do to claim jumpers!"

Chapter Ten

JEOPARDY FROM A STRANGER

The sight of the old man running at them with a raised ax handle so surprised Josh that he stood momentarily frozen in place beside Tyler.

But suddenly, Josh found his voice. "Wait, mister!" he cried. "Our plane crashed! We need help!"

"Don't lie to me!" the man shouted. "You're trying to steal my gold! Well, I'll stop that!"

Tyler exclaimed, "You hear that plane? They're looking for us! We've got to signal them before—"

"It's no use!" Josh interrupted in a low voice as the old prospector neared them. "We've got to get away. You go that way, I'll go this way! Meet at the pontoon! Now!"

Josh spun to his left and raced through the trees. He heard Tyler running in the opposite direction and the man's frustrated and angry shouts to stop.

Dodging through the stand of spruce, Josh risked a quick glance over his shoulder. The man was chasing Tyler. Josh cut back sharply toward the place where they had left the airplane float. *I've got to signal that plane before it flies away!* he thought. *But how?*

Panting from his hard run, Josh burst through the last of the forest and onto the small, rocky beach where the pontoon waited. With only a quick glance to assure himself that it was still there, Josh turned his face to the sky and used his hand to shield his eyes from the rain. The plane was only a tiny speck of movement in the distance.

Oh, no! Josh thought. He knew it was useless, but he waved both hands frantically as the steady drone of the single-engine aircraft vanished into the overcast.

For a moment, disappointment crushed down on him like a huge weight. His head dropped to his chest. He closed his eyes and tried to keep from groaning aloud. Then he forced his head up.

Come back! he cried to himself, gazing into the distance where the plane had disappeared. *Come back! Oh, please come back!*

He listened intently, but the sound of the plane had been swallowed up in the vast, soaring wilderness of silent mountains and trees.

Tyler! Josh suddenly thought. Spinning around, he scanned the dense forest, but there was no sight or sound of the other boy or the man with the ax handle.

Josh tried to be hopeful, expecting to see Tyler come running out of the trees at any moment. But there was nothing except a raven calling somewhere deep in the woods.

Then, faintly, as from a great distance, Josh thought he heard the plane again. Maybe it was coming back. If it did, how could he let the pilot know where he and the others were?

In the local newspapers, he had read about other survivors who had used rocks or tree limbs to spell out HELP or SOS on a sand or gravel bar. But the tiny strip where the boys had beached their pontoon was too small for that.

Smoke! Josh had also read that three signal fires meant someone needed help, but he had nothing with which to make even one fire. *What about a mirror to reflect sun into the plane?* Josh wondered. But it was raining, and he had nothing reflective anyway.

He thought of Mr. Ashby, the copilot, suffering on the island, and the fact that none of the survivors had heat or food. *If that plane comes back,* Josh told himself fiercely, *I've got to attract the pilot's attention. But how?*

And what about Tyler? He should have returned to the pontoon by now—if he isn't lost, and if the man with the ax handle hasn't caught him. Josh frantically looked around the trees, but there was no sign of the other boy.

I can't just stand here, Josh scolded himself. *I've got to decide what to do! But which is right? Try to help Tyler, or wait to signal the plane?* The question disturbed Josh, echoing in his mind until it was almost painful.

* * *

Tank peered anxiously out the plane's window, but the rain continued to splatter against it. The wind generated by the plane's movement through the air herded the drops into little rivulets that were forced backward along the glass. The dark sky matched Tank's mood.

He deeply regretted the angry words he had said to Josh about Alicia. The words sneaked out of the recesses of Tank's memory and haunted him. "She talks to you all the time and ignores me," he had told his best friend. "And when I try to say anything, she looks at me as if I didn't make any sense."

Tank frowned, recalling that when Josh had said he didn't think that was true, Tank had snapped, "Well, she does!" He had added, "Why can't she just leave us alone? We've been friends since we were babies, and we don't need anyone else—especially her."

Seconds later, Tank had turned around and left Josh, Alicia, and her father. *That seems so long ago and so unreal,* Tank thought. But those were about the last words he had ever said to Josh, who might now be hurt somewhere below in the rainy Alaskan wilderness.

Alicia's voice interrupted Tank's melancholy reflections. "It's really frustrating, isn't it?" she said.

"Yeah," he replied. "It's getting harder and harder to see clearly."

Alicia raised her voice. "Daddy, how are you doing?"

Mr. Wharton had left one corner of his earphone up so he could hear his passengers if they spoke. "Another couple of passes and we'll be done searching our grid," he reported.

"Then what?" Tank asked in alarm.

"We'll have to turn back to Anchorage."

"No!" Tank cried. "We can't! We've got to find Josh and the others!"

The pilot twisted in his seat to look directly at the boy. "We've been at this a long time now," he said, "and we don't even know if their plane went down in our sector."

Alicia protested, "But Tank's right! We can't give up! If they're down there, we've got to find them!"

"It's a decision that's out of our hands," her father said. "We're getting low on fuel."

Tank and Alicia exchanged concerned glances before she turned to her father again and asked, "How much is left?"

"Enough to stay on station for another few minutes," he replied, banking the aircraft to the left. "Then we'll need the rest to make it back to Merrill Field. We don't want to get forced down ourselves."

Tank watched the tip of the wing dip as the plane turned. "We're heading back toward that big lake that we passed a couple of minutes ago," Mr. Wharton said. "Josh's plane had floats, so maybe they landed on a lake like that."

"I thought of that," Alicia replied. "But I didn't any sign of the plane."

Or wreckage, Tank thought, and immediately he berated himself for thinking such a thing. He frowned and leaned his forehead against the window to look down as the plane leveled out.

What if there is no wreckage? he asked himself. *Suppose it sank?* He shook his head. *No, it wouldn't have gone down without a trace. Something would have broken off—I think.*

Three islands began drifting into sight as Mr. Wharton cleared the last mountain and dropped down to give the two observers the best possible view.

"Pretty dense forests down there," Alicia said. "They're so thick it would be almost impossible to spot anything in them."

Tank nodded absently, his gaze sweeping over the water and then focusing on the first two, smaller islands now coming up fast under his side of the plane.

Alicia added, "Maybe we're missing something. If the pilot had trouble and needed to decide where to land, he certainly would have tried for a nice open stretch of water like this. But if it sank—"

"Don't say that!" Tank snapped, twisting in his seat to glare at her.

She protested, "I only meant that we shouldn't overlook that possibility. But even if it did sink, everyone might have gotten to shore. Maybe to the mainland, or to one of those islands."

"Yeah," Tank said, trying to feel hopeful again. "Look for smoke. If they got ashore, they would build a fire, wouldn't they?"

"If they could," Alicia agreed. "Hey! There's smoke!"

"Where?"

"Beyond that bigger island on the mainland!" She pointed.

Tank couldn't see out his window, so he unbuckled his seat belt and strained to look out Alicia's side. "Show me!" he said, leaning across her so his face was near her window. "Show me fast!"

She pointed ahead, over the wing, to the mainland. "See it? That's smoke! Maybe a signal fire!"

In their excitement, neither Tank nor Alicia noticed the largest island on the other side of the plane, where three men frantically waved and shouted.

* * *

Josh had left the pontoon on the tiny beach and circled back to where the man with the ax handle had surprised the boys. From there, Josh followed the man's big boot prints in the mud until they caught up with Tyler's smaller ones. Then Josh moved even more carefully, looking back and forth at both the terrain ahead and the ground at his feet.

Soon he came upon a small, sliding footprint where Tyler had apparently tripped on a low-growing alder clump. Two handprints showed where Tyler had tried to break his fall. It looked as if he'd scrambled along on his hands and knees for a few feet, probably trying to regain his footing. Then . . .

Josh closed his eyes, but he couldn't erase the sight of the man's big prints and Tyler's smaller ones continuing on together. *He caught Tyler!* Josh had no doubt that his frightening thought was correct. *But where did they go?*

Thinking quickly, Josh decided, *It's logical that he would take Tyler to the cabin. So instead of following their tracks and maybe getting myself caught, I'd better move off to one side and try to find a different route to the cabin.*

Josh raised his eyes and was rewarded with the sight of a thickening column of smoke above the tree tops. *Of course!* Josh nodded with satisfaction. *They're in the cabin, so the man built up the fire. That's why there's more smoke now than—*

His train of thought was broken by another sound from above. *The plane!* Josh's gaze shot skyward past the dense stand of trees. *It's coming in across the island! If I can get to the shore in time, maybe they'll see me!*

Josh spun around and ran as hard as he could toward the sound of the approaching plane.

* * *

As the plane passed over, Tank exclaimed, "The smoke is getting darker! Maybe the survivors are putting something in the fire to make it burn black so we can see it."

"No," Alicia replied, "it's from a cabin! See over that last clump of trees? There's a shack in that clearing, but nobody's in sight. Not even a dog."

Tank groaned in disappointment. He pushed himself away from Alicia's side and plopped heavily into his own seat. "Not a signal fire from Josh and the others. It's just somebody's little cabin!"

In his frustration, Tank didn't even look out his own window as the pilot tilted the nose up and began to climb.

"Time for only one more pass," Mr. Wharton said, turning to look at his two passengers. "Then we're homeward bound."

* * *

Josh was running frantically through the dense forest when the small plane passed low and directly overhead.

"Hey!" Josh shouted, stopping to wave both hands and jump up and down. "Down here! We're here!"

He didn't quit his wild hopping until the plane's nose tilted upward and the aircraft began climbing and banking away toward the nearest mountain ridge.

They're gone for good! Josh thought. His body sagged like a leaking balloon, and his mind flooded with bitter regrets over the way he and Tank had parted. His best friend's hurt and angry words haunted Josh.

He recalled having tried to smooth things over when Tank had demanded, "Why are you always taking her side?" And Tank's final, angry words on the trail clanged in Josh's mind like huge brass bells: "Then you run and catch up with her, and have a great ol' time! I'm going back. Now, leave me alone!"

With an effort, Josh forced that sad memory into the background and focused on the present. He could no longer hear the plane, leading him to believe it had left the area.

The thought sickened him, especially when he knew Mr. Ashby was in dire need of medical attention. The copilot didn't even have a fire to keep him warm. If the weather got worse, the survivors might all end up like the original people who had given Terror Island its awful name. And Tyler was probably a prisoner of the old prospector.

The easy thing, Josh realized, was to save himself. After all, Tyler had been a lot of trouble ever since they met. Josh tried to tell himself that he didn't owe Tyler anything, that he could paddle the pontoon back to the island and the men.

But there was nothing Josh could do over there. Here, he could try to help Tyler. Josh tried to tell himself that the prospector wouldn't hurt Tyler. Maybe the man would just scare him, then let him go. *But what if he doesn't?* Josh thought.

Josh was sure that sooner or later, the prospector would try again to capture him. If he succeeded, what would happen to a couple of helpless boys in this wilderness?

Slowly straightening to his full height, Josh took a deep breath and turned away from the lake shore. As fast as he dared, he followed the smoke toward the prospector's cabin.

In a few minutes, he came to a clearing where all the spruce trees had been removed, leaving only some graceful birches. In the center stood a one-room cabin with a steeply pitched roof to help winter snows slide off. Nearby was an outhouse and a cache* on stilts to protect the old man's meat supply from hungry predators.

The fragrance of burning firewood made Josh shiver in his still-damp clothing. He had a momentary longing to be inside with Tyler, close to the stove.

Josh quickly rejected that thought and studied the cabin, wondering how to rescue Tyler. It was a plain structure made of logs. The end nearest to Josh had a narrow door and one small window. A huge rack of moose antlers was secured above the door. Two steel traps and a small animal hide turned inside out decorated the small area between the door and the side of the house.

Mustn't let him see me, Josh warned himself as he bent almost double and circled away, desperately trying to make himself invisible behind the white-barked birch trees. He passed old pieces of mining machinery rusting in the yard until he got a side view of the cabin.

There, one medium-size window had been cut in the logs. Josh wondered if there was another like it on the opposite side. The chimney at the far end of the cabin suggested there probably wasn't room enough for a window or door there.

So the only way in or out is through that single door or a window, Josh summarized mentally. *But how do I get Tyler out without that man grabbing me, too?*

Suddenly, the door seemed almost to explode outward, and the man charged straight toward Josh. The boy turned to run, but a strong hand clamped down on his wrist. In an instant, a steel-like arm curled around his chest.

"Got you!" the man shouted triumphantly.

Josh started struggling, but he was lifted from his feet and carried, kicking and yelling, toward the door. That's when he heard the plane coming back.

Chapter Eleven

HOW TERROR ISLAND REALLY GOT ITS NAME

Tank stared gloomily out the rain-streaked window as the pilot made his turn over the mountains prior to heading back across the lake for a final run. Then, if they saw nothing below, their low fuel would require them to abandon the search and head for home. Tank sighed with discouragement.

"There's still a chance, Tank," Alicia said.

He glanced toward her and tried to nod in agreement, but after a morning of looking, another couple of minutes to search didn't offer much hope. Still, Tank sharpened his focus to study the valley below the aircraft. Then the land ended and they were over water.

Each pass had taken the plane parallel to the area last searched. This time they didn't fly over the three islands but off to the right.

Tank's gaze skimmed along below, but his thoughts were back in the Chugach, where he had lost his temper over Josh and Alicia's friendship. Tank now realized he was the only one responsible for the rift between them. Josh had a right to

113

have other friends—even Alicia. But Tank hadn't wanted to share *any* of Josh's friendship.

That was wrong, Tank told himself. *Very wrong.* He closed his eyes to blot out the vision of him walking away from Josh back in the Chugach, and later refusing to see him after they got home. *Now,* Tank realized, *Josh might never come home again.*

Mr. Wharton asked above the steady sound of the engine, "You kids see anything down there?"

"Nothing yet," Alicia answered.

Tank opened his eyes and glanced below. The plane seemed to be traveling much faster down low than it did when it was high in the sky. The lake was a dark gray, reflecting the gloomy skies and Tank's mood.

"I don't see anything, either," he said loudly enough for the pilot to hear.

"We're coming up on the mainland again," Mr. Wharton announced. "Take one final good look in those trees before I take her back up and head for home."

The last of the lake slipped by below, and a small beach came into view off to Tank's left. He suddenly tensed and exclaimed, "What's that?"

Alicia asked, "What do you see?"

Tank didn't answer right away. He concentrated his gaze on something resting on the shoreline. He followed it with his eyes as the aircraft passed over it and the nose tilted, starting to climb.

"Well?" Alicia asked a bit anxiously.

"I saw something," he said, trying to identify it in his mind as trees flashed by below.

"Wreckage?" Alicia asked.

"No, it didn't look like an airplane. It was smaller than that. Anyway, there were no people, just this . . . thing."

Mr. Wharton asked, "What did it look like?"

"I didn't get a real good look, but it was man-made. I'm sure of that. It was sort of like a canoe or kayak, only lots bigger. Mr. Wharton, can you go around again so I can take another look?"

"This fuel gauge tells me we had better hightail it for home," he answered, "but we can make a very short run over that area again."

"Thanks." Tank glanced at Alicia while the plane banked sharply away from the mainland and headed back over the lake.

"Please," he whispered. "Oh please, let Josh be okay!"

* * *

The sound of an approaching airplane made Josh almost frantic to escape, but the prospector's grip was unbreakable. He shoved Josh hard, propelling him headlong into the cabin. Josh tried to keep his balance and avoid falling into the barrel stove* set against the back wall. It was burning so hot that the room was almost unbearable. Josh caught a glimpse of Tyler sitting dejectedly on the floor, his back against a wall insulated with flattened cardboard boxes.

Josh whirled to face his captor. "Look, mister!" he cried, "did you hear what I said? That plane is looking for us! We've got to signal—"

"You don't got to do nothin' o' the kind!" the man interrupted harshly. He closed the door behind him and took a couple of quick steps to touch Tyler's foot with his own calf-high laced boots. "I caught you two tryin' to jump my claim, and that gives me the right to deal with you proper-like."

"Please, mister—" Josh began again.

"Mister Zeke Dalton—that's me. Gold prospector, trapper, hunter, and . . ." he lowered his voice to add in a confidential tone, "a little strange in the head. Leastwise, that's what some folks believe. But me, I don't care what others say. I'm my own man, you hear?"

Nodding, Josh tried again. "Mr. Dalton, our plane crashed over there off that big island, and that plane you hear coming this way is looking for us."

"Is they more than you two young punks?" Mr. Dalton asked with sudden interest. "Men or boys?"

"Four men, and one is badly hurt. They haven't had a fire or food or any medical attention since—"

"More claim jumpers!" Zeke roared. "I shoulda knowed that right off! Well, just you wait. I'll fix 'em so's they won't try to steal no honest man's gold. Where you think you're a-goin'?"

Josh had started to sneak toward the door, but the moment his body tensed to run, Zeke was upon him again. He grabbed Josh by one arm and swung him around, smashing him into the wall.

"Now then, by thunder," Zeke shouted, "you try that again and I'll whack you so hard you'll land in the middle of next week!"

Josh didn't reply but looked helplessly toward the ceiling as the sound of the airplane passed overhead.

Across the room, a sob erupted from Tyler.

* * *

Mr. Wharton had climbed higher than before to make his turn over the mountains and head back across the lake. He called over his shoulder, "I've gained a little more altitude than before because I want to make a steeper descent. That will hopefully give me a little better opportunity to check out what you saw."

Tank heard the engine revving up as the nose dropped sharply.

Mr. Wharton added, "In a moment, I'm going down as close to the water as I dare."

Tank didn't reply but started looking ahead out the window, trying to see the tiny beach from as far out over the lake as possible.

Alicia released her seat restraints and leaned over to look across the top of Tank's head. "There's nothing to see on my side," she told him. "I'll help you look."

The pilot raised his voice again. "We're almost there. I see something. I'll try to make it out before I have to pull up."

Tank licked his dry lips as the plane's speed increased over the lake. He gave a little involuntary gasp when the plane's downward slant was abruptly changed and the nose tipped up. The engine roared as the plane climbed and banked, giving the observers an unobstructed view of the shore below.

"What do you see?" Mr. Wharton called.

Tank and Alicia both stared out the window at a strange object on the tiny beach. Then the plane flashed over the trees and the shoreline fell behind.

Alicia asked, "What do you think it was, Tank?"

He didn't immediately reply but searched his brain for something to match what had slid by below them. Nothing clicked as the plane reached for the rainy sky and headed back for Anchorage.

* * *

Josh sat on the floor with his knees drawn up before him and his back against the wall. He raised his eyes, moaning inwardly as he followed the sound of the aircraft until it faded away. Then, sick at heart, he turned toward Tyler, who sat with his head between his knees, utterly dejected.

The strange, old prospector began sharpening a long-bladed knife on a whetstone. Josh tried not to think about what that meant. Instead, he focused on how to escape.

He began by looking carefully around the cabin. The walls were devoid of pictures, calendars, or other homelike touches. Instead, nails had been indiscriminately hammered in and draped with shirts, hats, pieces of leather, and other objects that suggested the owner was not a tidy housekeeper.

The only escape, Josh decided, was through the single door or either of the two side windows. But they were too small for a hasty exit, and besides, even if they were broken out, sharp pieces might remain.

The boys' captor blocked the door, which had winter coats, gloves, and caps hanging on it. Josh noticed that the old man regarded them carefully. There was a fierceness in his watery, blue eyes and a stubborn set to his long, white-bearded chin. Josh knew that Zeke Dalton was not thinking kindly about the boys.

"I reckon leavin' you for the wolves would be best," Zeke mused aloud. He gingerly tested the knife edge with his left hand. The index finger was missing.

Josh declared stoutly, "My father says that wolves are very shy and don't attack people."

"Oh, he does, does he?" Zeke growled as he slipped the knife into a sheath on his belt. "Well, you boys might just find out about that soon enough. 'Course, I could leave you both over near where I seen a sow grizzly with twin cubs. A grizzly mother ain't afraid of nothin' or nobody! She'll attack you boys on sight."

Josh blinked, keenly aware of just how dangerous it was to be anywhere near a mother bear and her young.

Zeke noticed and exclaimed, "Yes sireee! A grizzly! That way, even if someone was to ever find your ornery bones, ol' Zeke would be in the clear!"

Josh tried to suppress a shudder, but Zeke didn't see it

because Tyler made an anguished sound that brought the old man's eyes to the other boy. Steam rose from Tyler's damp clothing where the intense heat was drying them out for the first time since the plane went down.

"Scared, huh?" Zeke asked Tyler. "Can't say as I blame you none. A bear maulin' is a mighty fearsome thing." He turned back to Josh. "You say you got more claim jumpers on that big island?"

"Not claim jumpers. There's a pilot, a couple of park rangers, and a fish and game officer. Mister Zeke, one of them —Tyler's uncle—is badly hurt. They have no medicine—"

"You done told me that!" Zeke interrupted, waving his hand in dismissal of the thought. "That won't matter none pretty soon. That there is called Terror Island. You know why, punk?"

"My name is Josh Ladd. Yes, I know why the island is called that. Another plane crashed there some time back, and the people weren't found before they died of hypothermia."

"That's only partly right, Josh," Zeke sneered. "A grizzly got two of—"

"Stop it!" Tyler yelled, scrambling to his feet. "Stop it, I say! It's bad enough to be trapped in here, but you don't have to talk that way!"

"You got spunk, Tyler," Zeke answered gruffly. "Not that it's goin' to help none."

"Mister Zeke," Josh said, "please leave him alone."

The watery, old, blue eyes turned upon Josh. "You his best friend?"

Josh hesitated. "We're friends."

A crafty look came over Zeke's whiskered face. "I jist got me another good idee. Suppose I was to let one of you go. Which should it be?"

Josh and Tyler exchanged glances across the stove, but neither spoke.

"Think about it," Zeke urged, a tinge of glee in his tone. "One of you goes free. He gets back to them others on that island, and everybody hopes to git saved by some airplane. The other punk stays here with me until I put him out with the wolves and the bears."

Josh felt his heart start to speed up. *What people said about these hermits is right,* Josh thought. *He's been out here alone so long that he's not right in the head.*

"We're both going," Josh said firmly. "You don't really want to hurt two kids like us. We didn't do anything to you, and we're certainly not after your gold. We just want to get home to our families."

"Families?" Zeke repeated. "You got families?"

"Parents, sisters and brothers, some friends—" Josh began, but the old man cut him off.

"Friends? Family? Mine run me off years ago! Said I was no good! Told me to go off and never come back! Well, that's what I done. But I don't need no family or friends! I only need myself."

He paused, frowning, then held up his mutilated hand. "Why, the only thing I couldn't do was sew my finger back on when I accidently whacked it with a hatchet. Now, comin' back to what I asked before: Which one of you wants to go free, and which one stays with me?"

* * *

Tank raised his voice so the pilot could hear him. "Did you get a good look at that thing when we passed over it?" he asked.

"A quick glance was all," Mr. Wharton replied, "but I think it might have been a pontoon, an airplane float."

Tank and Alicia stared at the pilot as he swiveled his head to look back at his passengers.

"Yes!" Mr. Wharton exclaimed. "I think that's it! It could have happened when the plane hit the water. One float broke off, and the other sank with . . ." He checked himself and turned to look out the windshield again.

Tank's mouth went dry at the pilot's unspoken words. Tank tried to ignore the thought that snapped into his mind, but it was useless.

If the plane sank that fast, probably nobody had a chance to get out.

Tank shoved the thought aside and shouted, "Mr. Wharton, we've got to go back! We've got to take another look! Maybe they're down there and we didn't see them!"

"I'm already turning," the pilot replied. "Then, regardless of what we see, we've got to head for home or we'll be lucky to get back to Anchorage."

Tank faced Alicia, who had returned to her seat. "You scared?"

"To death," she replied as the plane banked sharply and turned back toward the lake. "For us and them."

Impulsively reaching over, Tank clutched her hand. He suggested nervously, "Let's say a prayer."

Chapter Twelve

A RUN FOR LIFE

The old prospector grinned with delight at his idea. "Well?" he said, glancing from Josh to Tyler. "Which one o' you young punks wants to go free while I put the other out fer the bears and wolves?"

Tyler exclaimed, "I'll go!" He started to rise, but Zeke pushed him back down.

"You're too anxious," he declared. "You stay. The other one goes." Stepping to the door, the prospector opened it and motioned to Josh. "Now git!"

Josh glanced at Tyler and saw the desperation in his eyes. With all his heart, Josh wanted to escape from this strange old man, but the silent terror on Tyler's face was too much for him.

"Thanks, Mr. Zeke," he said, surprised at his own calm words, "but Tyler knows how to paddle back to the others on the island. I don't. So please let him—"

"No!" Zeke roared. "You go!" He grabbed Josh's arm and slung him through the door and into the open air. "Not that it'll make that much diff'rence," Zeke called after him, "'cause as quick as I tie up this other punk, I'm a comin' after you. I'll ketch you before you git far. Then you'll both face them wild animals, but at least I done give you both a chance by lettin' you go. Now, git movin'!"

* * *

Mr. Wharton completed his turn and flew back low across the lake. He called, "Take a good look at both the island and the mainland where we saw that broken float."

Wordlessly, Tank and Alicia pressed their faces close to their respective windows. Tank strained to see some sign of life as they skimmed between the largest island and the two smaller ones.

He was so tense that he jumped when Alicia spoke. "Dad! Look!" she said. "On the big island! People!"

Tank quickly unbuckled his safety harness and leaned over her shoulder to see.

"Yes!" he cried. "Three . . . no, four men waving at us!" One was sitting down, but the others were jumping up and down and wildly waving bright orange life jackets.

Tank and Alicia waved back as Mr. Wharton flew his aircraft directly in front of the four men. Their mouths opened wide in silent shouts.

"Tank, take your seat!" the pilot said. "I'm going to dip my wings to make sure they know we saw them!"

"I don't see Josh!" Tank exclaimed, dropping back into his place. "Maybe those guys aren't from his plane!"

"That's the only aircraft reported missing," Mr. Wharton replied. "There's no sign of their plane, but those people have got to be the ones we're looking for."

"Then where's Josh?" Tank cried in anguish.

Alicia tried to sound hopeful. "He's probably out of sight under those trees."

"Yeah," Tank replied, "I hope you're right." He raised his voice. "I'm buckled in, Mr. Wharton."

"Good! Here we go!" The pilot dipped both wings as the plane passed the end of the island and began climbing. He added, "They'll know that we can't land because this isn't a float plane. They can't guess we're low on fuel, but I hope they understand that we're not abandoning them."

Tank asked, "Are we heading home, Mr. Wharton?"

"We've got no choice," he replied. "But I'm sure those men will know that I'll radio their position so a helicopter can be sent to pick them up."

Those men, Tank mused. *Not those men and Josh.*

Tank closed his eyes and rested his head against the cold window while a fearful thought sliced through him. *I hope Josh didn't go down with the plane!*

* * *

A few minutes before, Josh had stood outside Zeke Dalton's open cabin door. He pretended not to notice that Tyler's body was shaking with fright at the fearsome prospect of being left alone again with the strange old man.

Tyler pleaded, "Don't leave me, Josh!"

Tyler had caused Josh a lot of grief, and yet it was Tyler's skill that got the boys across the lake on the airplane float. It wasn't his fault that they hadn't found someone to help them. And it certainly wasn't Tyler's fault that the boys had run into a hostile old recluse.

"I'll get the men and be back for you," Josh said.

It was a gallant promise that Josh wasn't sure he could carry out, but he would try.

Zeke yelled, "If you make it, I'll be a-waitin' fer them other claim jumpers, too, an' with more than an ax handle! A man's got a right to pertect his gold! Now, git goin'!"

As Josh turned to obey, the prospector added with a wicked grin, "Don't fergit to watch out for that mean ol' grizzly sow I told you about!"

His mocking laughter followed Josh as he stood among the graceful birch trees outside the cabin. He glanced around to get his bearings. *That way,* he decided. *That's where we left the pontoon and our life jackets.*

He started running toward the forest that surrounded the shack. As he passed the prospector's pile of sawed and stacked firewood, Josh glimpsed a two-seated kayak and a set of double-bladed paddles leaning against the far end of the pile. He remembered his futile efforts to paddle the airplane float before Tyler had taken over the task. Josh feared that he still couldn't steer the pontoon back to the island, so he veered toward the kayak.

"Hey!" Zeke yelled, poking his head out the door, the ax

handle raised over his head, "git away from there! My ol' pardner an' me made that afore he got hisself drowned."

Josh abandoned the kayak idea and began running through the spruce forest, dodging dense alder clumps. He glanced back and saw Zeke leaving the cabin, securing the door behind him. *He's not giving me much of a head start,* Josh mused, trying not to fall on the slippery ground.

He had run about a hundred yards when an idea popped into his head: *Mr. Zeke will remember I mentioned getting here on a pontoon. He'll think I'm going there, so he won't expect me to circle back to free Tyler.*

Still running, Josh made a hasty plan. If he could dodge Zeke and return to the cabin, he and Tyler could take the two-man kayak from the woodpile and carry it to the lake. After they shoved off, Zeke couldn't follow them, because the water was too cold to swim.

First, I've got to fool him about where I'm going, but how? Josh quickly looked ahead and to both sides. On the left, a tangle of low-growing alder clumps on a small ridge offered a possible brief hiding place. Beyond that, through the trees, he noticed a gravel bar about six feet wide and a couple of hundred yards long. It extended from the shore into the lake like a finger.

Josh's glance slid off the bar to focus on the alder clumps. *Yes!* he told himself with satisfaction, *that should work! But Mr. Zeke mustn't see me turn back toward the cabin.*

Josh was panting hard when he spotted a downed spruce log ahead. Glancing over his shoulder, he was relieved that he couldn't see Zeke. Hopefully, that meant Zeke couldn't see him either.

Now! he told himself, puffing with exertion. Instead of jumping over the log and continuing toward the lake, he leaped up on it and ran along it to the left. Bounding off the far end, he dropped out of sight among the sheltering alders.

Breathing hard but quietly, Josh waited. *This had better work!* he thought. *If he sees me, it's all over.*

* * *

Mr. Wharton's plane was still climbing as Tank glumly recalled the scene they were leaving behind. Four men had waved life jackets. One of those men had not been standing, which suggested he was injured. There had been no sign of a tent, fire, or the nuisance bear they had been flying to a new location. Just four men, but no Josh.

A hand gently placed on his arm snapped Tank out of his reverie. He turned to meet Alicia's eyes. "You've got to believe we'll find him," she said.

"I know. But I'm scared for Josh."

"At least we know where the others are. Daddy will radio their position as soon as he levels out. A helicopter will be sent to help. They'll find Josh, and he'll be okay. You'll see."

Tank nodded, wanting to believe that, but he knew that not everyone survived an air crash. He blinked at the sunlight when the plane broke through the clouds. Immense Alaskan mountain peaks stood majestically on both sides of the plane. The sun glistened on snow still clinging to the crevices.

Alaska was a truly spectacular place, but it was also dangerous.

Tank watched the pilot reach for the microphone and speak into it. "This is November Seven One Zero Golf. I have a sighting."

Tank asked in a low voice, "What's he saying?"

"He's identified our plane to the RCC and notified them that we've found Josh's plane."

Nodding, Tank recalled that RCC meant the Rescue Coordination Center at Elmendorf Air Force Base. He listened as Alicia's father again transmitted, giving the coordinates where the four survivors and airplane float had been sighted.

He continued, "RCC, I'm low on fuel and returning to Merrill Field. Please advise when a rescue unit will be dispatched to the crash site."

Tank leaned back in his seat and sighed deeply as Mr. Wharton relayed further details of the sighting to the RCC.

Alicia assured him, "We did everything we could. We found them. Soon this will all be over, and Josh will be safe. Then all three of us can be friends." She paused before adding, "I mean, if that's all right with you."

Tank silently regarded her for a long moment. Earlier, it had been easy to blame her for his conflict with Josh. It had even seemed that somehow it was Alicia' fault that Josh had flown off with a tranquilized bear and had been in a plane crash.

For the first time he could remember, he and Josh had not been together on an adventure. Now they might be separated for good. The bad memories of how he and Josh had parted could haunt him forever. But certainly none of that was Alicia's fault.

Finally Tank reached out, touched her hand, and said, "Anything's all right with me if only we get Josh back safely."

Mr. Wharton turned to look over his shoulder. He grinned broadly and said, "The air force is dispatching a chopper for those people, but a CAP pilot in a float plane flying the Beta grid next to us radioed that he could be on site in a few minutes."

Alicia cried happily, "That's wonderful!"

"There's more," her father continued. "He doesn't have room for four passengers, but the RCC gave him permission to land, render first aid, and pick up the man who appeared to be injured. The helicopter will bring in the others."

"Great!" Alicia exclaimed, turning to grip Tank's arm excitedly. "That means all of them will soon be on their way back to Anchorage."

"Yeah, great!" Tank replied, then added softly, "If only Josh is among them."

* * *

In the alder clump, Josh carefully raised his head and tried to control his heavy breathing. Peering through the branches, he watched Zeke step over the log, still carrying his ax handle. He seemed so sure of catching Josh that he wasn't running.

Good! Josh thought as the old prospector continued away from him. *He didn't see me. He's not even trying to follow my muddy footprints.* Josh shook his head as Zeke drifted off to the right. *He must have lost my trail. He won't find me or the float over that way.*

When Zeke had gone far enough ahead for Josh to feel safe, he slowly rose and quietly turned back toward the cabin. He had gone only a few steps when a low, guttural growl made him stop dead in his tracks.

He glanced around wildly, expecting to see the mother grizzly and twin cubs Zeke had warned about. Instead, he saw a big black bear crawl out of the lake and onto the small beach where the boys had left the float.

It can't be, Josh told himself, *but it looks like the same bear from the plane!*

The animal shook itself like a dog, throwing water in a great spray. Then the bear sniffed noisily, let out another growl, and bounded forward, mouth open wide to pounce on something Josh couldn't see.

Josh frowned. *What's he doing?* he wondered.

The bear's head snapped up, and one of the boys' life jackets sailed through the air. Great forepaws next swatted down at something, making a strange sound. Josh frowned, then recognized it. *The pontoon! He must smell where Tyler and I were sitting. He's wrecking it!*

That left the two-man kayak as the only way back to the island. Josh slipped away as quietly as possible from the alders, heading in the direction of the cabin. The bear roared, making Josh glance back in time to see it stand up on its hind legs and sniff the air.

I think it's caught my scent! Josh thought, and he broke into a wild run toward the safety of the cabin.

He glanced back over his shoulder to see how fast the bear was gaining on him. He stopped and blinked in surprise when he realized the animal was running off through the trees at an angle. *He's not after me! He must smell Mr. Zeke!*

Josh looked to the old man. He was still moving off to the right, his back to the approaching danger. *What's the matter with him?* Josh wondered. *Can't he hear that bear coming up behind him?*

Josh stood uncertainly, watching the bear bounding toward the unsuspecting prospector. Josh wanted to shout a warning, but that would surely attract the bear's attention. He would then come after Josh, and he had no weapon. But then, Zeke's ax handle wouldn't do much good against a bear, either.

Josh suddenly cocked his head at another sound. *The plane! It's coming back!* He glanced skyward, beyond the tips of the spruce trees, and felt a surge of hope. He couldn't see the aircraft, but the sound was drawing steadily nearer.

I've got to get in the open where they can see me before Zeke catches me again! he realized. Josh remembered the gravel bar. *That's the best place to be,* he thought, and he rose on tiptoes to run quietly, hoping the bear wouldn't notice him.

To be sure, Josh took another quick look toward the bear closing in on the old prospector. Josh was confident he could reach the gravel bar in time to signal the approaching plane.

But what would happen to Zeke?

Chapter Thirteen

DESPERATE MOMENTS

Josh slid to a stop, watching the bear bound toward the back of the unsuspecting old prospector. He was still carrying the ax handle but was walking more slowly now, as though wondering where the boy had gone.

Turn around! Josh silently urged. *Turn now!*

Zeke kept going, however, unaware that the bear had closed within 50 yards of him. Josh cupped his hands to shout a warning, but he hesitated when he heard the sound of the aircraft's engine change slightly.

Glancing up past the spruce trees to the glowering skies, Josh glimpsed a red-and-white, high-winged plane. It rapidly dropped lower over the dense forest beyond the prospector's cabin.

That's not the same plane I saw before! Josh realized with new hope. *That one had landing wheels, but this one has floats! It can land on the lake! I've got to get out where he can see me!*

Josh was ready to start running toward the gravel bar, but another quick glance at the prospector held the boy in his tracks. The bear was closing ground rapidly.

Instantly, Josh cupped hands to his mouth and shouted, "Mr. Zeke! Turn around! Turn around!"

The recluse stopped abruptly, looked back, and recoiled at the sight of the bear.

Hearing Josh's voice, the animal slid to a halt on the muddy ground in front of the man, then spun around to face the boy.

The animal rose on its hind legs and loudly sniffed the air. Then, seeming to recognize Josh's scent, the bear started popping long, yellow teeth and growling menacingly.

"Uh oh!" Josh muttered. "Now I've done it!"

With every fiber of his being, he wanted to turn and flee, but he forced himself to stand still. He didn't want to further excite the already aggravated bear. He also vividly recalled this same black beast standing over him with open jaws before being driven off with bear spray. Now, however, there was no one around with any defense.

"Oh, Lord, help!" Josh whispered as the bear dropped back down on all fours and charged toward him.

Josh instinctively knew he had no choice now but to run. He turned and fled across the rain-soaked ground toward the gravel bar.

Could the approaching pilot see him and land in time to save him? *If not,* Josh thought as he ran, *what am I going to do?*

He was sure of one thing: He didn't intend to give up and let the bear maul him.

Vaguely, he heard Zeke shouting something, but Josh was too frightened to understand. He dashed through the spruce forest, trying not to stumble or fall. "Oh, Lord! Oh, Lord!" he heard himself praying between gasps for breath.

He dared not look back for fear of tripping over fallen tree limbs or other forest floor litter. He knew the bear's broad, flat paws and great strength allowed it to easily outrun any human being. From the sounds behind him, Josh guessed the animal was knocking down small brush that Josh had been forced to dodge around.

The old prospector was still shouting something when Josh neared the end of the forest. The flat finger of gravel bar stretched ahead of him. But then what? Neither Josh nor Zeke had an effective weapon. There was no one else to help. Even if Josh darted into the opening where the pilot could see him, the plane might not be able to land in time.

But I can't give up! Josh told himself again as he burst out of the trees and crunched onto the gravel. *Think! Think! There must be a way!*

With burning lungs gasping for air, Josh fled onto the long, narrow gravel bar. He risked a fleeting peek back. There was no sign of Zeke, but the bear burst out of the forest and bounded after him onto the gravel.

Josh's gaze shot skyward just as the aircraft zoomed low over the last of the forest, flying slightly to the right of the gravel bar, heading toward the big island.

"Hey!" Josh yelled so loudly his throat hurt. He desperately waved both hands over his head while trying to run backward. "Down here! Please look down!"

The aircraft was so low that Josh could see the pilot

peering down. His head swiveled to the left as though he were trying to look back at something.

"Hey! Hey!" Josh screeched, waving frantically as the plane drew even with him. "I think he saw me!" Josh shouted as the plane skimmed past, then suddenly nosed skyward. The wings wagged briefly from side to side, signaling recognition.

"Yes!" Josh shrieked in relief. "Thank God, he did see me! Now if he can circle back and land in time—"

Josh didn't finish the sentence because his eyes flashed back to the bear. It had stopped a few feet onto the gravel bar, less than 200 feet away. That distance could be covered in seconds.

Unless . . .

An idea popped into Josh's head as he watched the bear's massive head tilt up toward the plane. *He's afraid of it!* Josh realized. He turned his face upward and whispered, "Please make him come back—fast!"

A menacing growl snapped Josh's eyes back to the bear. It clicked its long teeth and charged across the gravel with short, puffing sounds. "Uf! Uf! Uf!"

Pivoting on his feet, Josh ran for his life toward the point where the gravel bar ended in the lake. He risked another glance at the sky and saw the plane had completed a tight turn beyond the islands.

He's coming back! But he won't get here in time unless I—

Josh spun around to face his adversary. Throwing up both arms, Josh shouted with all the power and fear in him.

The startled bear slowed, but only for a few seconds. With

another roar, it continued to charge.

Josh swung around once more and raced toward the lake. In seconds, he would reach it and have nowhere to go. His only hope was in the float plane, which was now flying at tree-top level, heading straight toward Josh.

At first, he thought the pilot was going to land on the lake, but the sound of the engine didn't ease off. Instead, it seemed to be going at full throttle.

Josh slowed at the end of the bar. He was trapped between the bear and the frigid water. But he put his final, desperate idea into action and turned to face the onrushing bear.

He jumped up and down, but instead of waving, he repeatedly and rapidly motioned with both arms toward the bear. "Stop him! Stop him!" he shouted, even though he knew the pilot couldn't hear him.

The approaching plane's spinning propeller made a silver arc in the air as the nose slanted down. Josh felt hopeful. *I think the pilot understands!* he thought. He continued his furious motions until the plane was close enough that Josh could see the pilot making rapid downward motions with one hand.

He wants me to get down! Josh realized. He threw himself flat on the gravel, unmindful of the rough stones gouging his hands. He glanced back at the bear. It slid to a stop barely 30 feet away, its eyes turned toward the aircraft. The plane roared low over Josh's outstretched body. He lifted his head and whooped loudly as the bear whipped around and fled back across the gravel bar toward the trees.

Josh hollered with joy as the aircraft pulled out of its dive and climbed skyward. "Thanks!" Josh shouted, leaping to his feet. "Whooeee! Thanks a million!"

He waved even though he knew the pilot probably couldn't see him now. Smiling and shaking his head in wonder, Josh swung his gaze to where the bear had disappeared into the trees. He thought happily, *I hope he scared that bear so much that it keeps running clear up to the North Pole!*

He turned a joyful face upward, where the plane's twin floats were visible as the craft approached for a landing on the lake. Josh quickly decided what he would do when the pilot eased over to pick him up. *I'll tell him to go help Tyler's uncle and the others while I go back for Tyler. Then we'll both—*

His thoughts were interrupted by the sound of someone walking on the gravel behind him. He whirled around. "Mr. Zeke!" he shouted.

The old prospector approached with the ax handle still gripped in his hand. Josh licked his suddenly dry lips and tried to swallow the lump that rose in his throat.

Zeke raised the ax handle. "This wouldn't-a done a lick o' good against that bear," he said, his words barely audible. "I didn't hear him comin' up behind me. If you hadn't sung out . . ." He left the sentence hanging in the air before adding, "Reckon you saved my ornery ol' hide."

Josh didn't say anything, but behind him, he heard the pilot cut the plane's engine and the twin floats touch the water, gliding toward the gravel bar.

The old man added thoughtfully, "After you hollered an' that bear took out after you, I figgered you was a goner fer sure." He glanced down at the ax handle. "Reckon I won't need this no more." He turned and tossed it into the lake on the far side of the gravel bar, away from the airplane.

"Now," he said with a smile, "do you want to git on that plane an' go across to your friends on the island, or do you want to come with me to free your friend?"

Josh grinned happily as the plane coasted near. "After I thank the pilot for driving off that bear and tell him where to find the others, I'll go with you to get Tyler. I think he'll be glad to see me."

* * *

Tank and Alicia and the families of all the survivors waited eagerly at Elmendorf Air Force Base for Josh and the others. A military helicopter had rescued all those the float plane hadn't been able to bring out. Tyler's uncle, Ross Ashby, would recover from his broken ribs. All the other survivors were going to be okay, too.

Josh had lost his video camera, but he still had a great story to tell. It would not only be written up in his father's publication, but it was sure to be featured in the local newspaper and other media as well.

"Here comes Tyler!" Alicia exclaimed as the boy walked toward them from the chopper.

Mr. Radburn rushed up to embrace his son.

"There's Josh!" Tank said as he and Alicia spotted him and the Ladd family surged forward to greet him.

Tank and Alicia stood nearby while Tank tried to think what he would say to Josh. Finally, Josh turned from his family and looked at Tank. For a moment, an awkward silence held them apart. Then Tank approached uneasily while Alicia held back. "I'm sorry, Josh," Tank said. His voice broke as he hastily added, "I was so wrong, and I'm awful sorry!"

Josh hugged him while the other people discreetly moved away. "It's okay," Josh said huskily. "It's over. Let's forget it."

Tank stepped back. "We're still friends?" he asked.

Josh grinned. "Still friends, and always will be."

"Thanks!" Tank gave Josh a friendly punch high on the arm.

Josh's eyes fell on Alicia. "What about you and her?" he asked in a low voice.

"Things are great between us! She and her father let me fly along in the search."

"That's what the helicopter crew told us," Josh replied. "You two found us, even though you didn't see me at the time. Come on. I want to thank her."

He and Tank walked together to Alicia. "Hi," Josh said. "Thanks for everything."

"You're welcome," she replied with a happy smile. "I'm glad everything turned out all right."

Tyler left his father and approached Josh, Tank, and Alicia. He hesitated, his face somber. "Is it okay if I join you?" he asked uncertainly.

When all three nodded at him, he turned to Josh. "What

you did back at the lake makes me ashamed that I ever called you a cheechako," he confessed. "I won't ever do that again." Before Josh could reply, Tyler blurted, "I'd like to be your friend, too."

Josh reached out to shake his hand. "Nobody can have too many friends," he said.

The others smiled broadly and nodded in agreement.

GLOSSARY

CHAPTER 1

Anchorage (ANK-er-age): Originally, steamships used to anchor offshore where a tent city of railroad workers started what is now Alaska's largest city. About half of the forty-ninth state's entire population lives here.

Chugach (CHEW-gatch) *State Park:* A state-operated wilderness of 495,000 acres close to urban areas. The park is home to such birds as bald eagles, fish such as spawning salmon, and animals, including porcupine, lynx, wolf, black and brown bears, moose, beaver, and wolverine.

Fireweed: In this story, it's a fictitious Alaskan community. In reality, fireweed is a plant that grows up to six feet tall and has bright pink blossoms. In late June, blooming begins on the lower stems, and the plant gradually blossoms all the way to the top by August or September. When fireweed "tops out," winter is close. Fireweed takes its name from deep horizontal roots that allow fast regrowth after a fire.

Moraine (muh-RAIN): An irregular mound of sand, gravel, clay, and boulders deposited by a glacier that once carried it.

Cheechako (chee-CHAW-koe): In Alaska, this means newcomer, tenderfoot, or greenhorn. It's the opposite of a sourdough, or old-timer.

CHAPTER 2

Malihini (mah-lee-HEE-nee): Hawaiian for newcomer.

Skookum (SKOO-kuhm): An Alaskan native word of high approval. It can mean brave, strong, or smart, depending on how it's used.

Sourdough (sour-doe): Originally, a yeasty, long-lived concoction early Alaskan pioneers and prospectors used to leaven bread and other baked goods. Now it more commonly means an old-time Alaska resident, especially a Bush resident.

CHAPTER 3

Banty (BAN-tee) *rooster:* Correctly called bantam and named after small domestic chickens that closely resemble standard breeds. The word is also used to describe a person of small stature, often with a combative nature.

Greenbelt: A narrow strip of land containing trees or other usually green plants, such as a park or farming land around a community.

Williwaw (willy-whaw): In this story, a dog named for the

strongest of Alaska's three most notorious winds. Williwaw's strong gusts can reach 115 miles per hour. The Chinook (SH-nook) is a warm winter wind that will melt ice or blow over power lines. Chinook is also another name for an Alaskan king salmon. Taku (tah-koo) is another gusting Alaskan wind with speeds up to more than 100 miles per hour. The name comes from a glacier in southeast Alaska.

CHAPTER 4

Knik (KAH-nick) *Arm:* An Alaskan body of water forming the northernmost arm of Cook Inlet. Knik Arm connects Anchorage to the Matanuska (matt-ah-NOOSE-kah) Valley.

Chop: A common term used by pilots to indicate rough air; from the short, abrupt motions made when a plane hits such air.

CHAPTER 5

Hypothermia (hi-poe-THERM-ee-ah): A life-threatening condition that can lead to death when the body's inner or core temperature drops below 95 degrees Fahrenheit.

CHAPTER 6

Giardia (gee-AR-dee-ah): Technically, giardiasis (gee-ar-DIE-ah-sis), a disease or infestation in human beings characterized by lower intestinal distress. Water, no matter how clear and clean looking, can be a source of the infestation.

CHAPTER 8

Kayak (KY-yack): Originating with the Eskimos, this is the term for a small boat with a thin cover on a light framework. A flexible closure around the occupant's waist keeps the craft watertight.

Cook Inlet: A 200-mile-long body of water extending from the Gulf of Alaska south of Homer all the way north past Anchorage to the Susitna (soo-SEAT-nah) Flats. The inlet was named for Captain James Cook, who explored the waters in 1778.

CHAPTER 9

Bush: Always capitalized in Alaska, the term refers to the countless small, remote villages in the state's vast wilderness. Some villages are accessible only by plane, dogsled, or snowmobile (which is called a snow machine in Alaska).

CHAPTER 10

Cache (kash): In Alaska, the word has two meanings: (1) tiny houses on stilts that hold food and keep it out of the reach of animals, as in this story; (2) a supply of food or other valuables, usually for emergencies.

CHAPTER 11

Barrel stove: A manufactured, cast-iron, wood-burning stove made from a 55-gallon oil drum turned on its side. Most of these are used for heating, but the one in this story has a flat top that can be used for cooking.

Don't Miss a Single "Ladd Family Adventure!"

Collect the entire series and follow Josh Ladd and his friends as they find their way in and out of danger. Each unique story combines nonstop action and suspense with unforgettable lessons about trusting in God.

Adrenaline-Pumping Alaskan Adventures

Hunted in the Alaskan Wilderness (#13)

After moving to Alaska, Josh and Tank must learn to trust God when they are tracked by a criminal and a ferocious bear.

Spine-Tingling Hawaiian Adventures

Panic in the Wild Waters (#12)

From tidal waves to sea turtle smugglers, the Ladds have their hands full in this exciting ocean adventure.

Case of the Dangerous Cruise (#11)

A dream cruise becomes a nightmare for Josh and Tank when they're caught up in a smuggling operation that threatens international peace!

Night of the Vanishing Lights (#10)

Josh and his pals set out to investigate strange lights atop Kamakou Peak and find trouble in the shadows.

Eye of the Hurricane (#9)

Josh and Tank race against time and a raging storm in search of Josh's father.

Terror at Forbidden Falls (#8)

Josh and his friends uncover a dangerous plot to detonate a nuclear device in Honolulu.

Peril at Pirate's Point (#7)

While getting help for Tank's injured father, Josh and Tank are captured by a pair of ruthless smugglers.

Mystery of the Wild Surfer (#6)

A young surfer saves Josh from drowning, but their friendship puts the entire family at risk.

Secret of the Sunken Sub (#5)

A fishing trip turns troublesome when Josh witnesses the sinking of a Soviet robot submarine and is pursued by Russian spies.

The Dangerous Canoe Race (#4)
Josh and his friends paddle into peril by racing a bully willing to do anything to win.

Mystery of the Island Jungle (#3)
Josh must find the courage to free his friend from a vicious stranger.

The Legend of Fire (#2)
Josh attempts to rescue his father from kidnappers and an erupting volcano.

Secret of the Shark Pit (#1)
The Ladds brave a life-or-death race for hidden treasure.

$5.99 each
Available at your favorite Christian bookstore.

4. Our Response: Receive Christ

We must trust Jesus Christ and receive Him by personal invitation.

The Bible Says ...

"Behold, I stand at the door and knock. If anyone hears My voice and opens the door, I will come in to him and dine with him, and he with Me." *Revelation 3:20, NKJV*

"But as many as received Him, to them He gave the right to become children of God, to those who believe in His name." *John 1:12, NKJV*

"If you confess with your mouth the Lord Jesus and believe in your heart that God has raised Him from the dead, you will be saved." *Romans 10:9, NKJV*

Are you here ... or here?

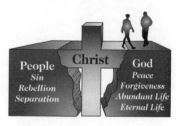

Is there any good reason why you cannot receive Jesus Christ right now?

How to Receive Christ:

1. Admit your need (say, "I am a sinner").
2. Be willing to turn from your sins (repent) and ask for God's forgiveness.
3. Believe that Jesus Christ died for you on the cross and rose from the grave.
4. Through prayer, invite Jesus Christ to come in and control your life through the Holy Spirit (receive Jesus as Lord and Savior).

What to Pray:

Dear Lord Jesus,
    I know that I am a sinner, and I ask for Your forgiveness. I believe You died for my sins and rose from the dead. I turn from my sins and invite You to come into my heart and life. I want to trust and follow You as my Lord and Savior.

In Your Name, Amen.

_____   _____
Date   Signature

GOD'S ASSURANCE: HIS WORD

IF YOU PRAYED THIS PRAYER,

THE BIBLE SAYS ...

"For, 'Everyone who calls on the name of the Lord will be saved.'" *Romans 10:13, NIV*

Did you sincerely ask Jesus Christ to come into your life? Where is He right now? What has He given you?

"For it is by grace you have been saved, through faith—and this not from yourselves, it is the gift of God—not by works, so that no one can boast." *Ephesians 2:8-9, NIV*

THE BIBLE SAYS ...

"He who has the Son has life; he who does not have the Son of God does not have life. These things I have written to you who believe in the name of the Son of God, that you may know that you have eternal life, and that you may continue to believe in the name of the Son of God." *1 John 5:12-13, NKJV*

Receiving Christ, we are born into God's family through the supernatural work of the Holy Spirit who indwells every believer. This is called regeneration or the "new birth."

This is just the beginning of a wonderful new life in Christ. To deepen this relationship you should:

1. Read your Bible every day to know Christ better.
2. Talk to God in prayer every day.
3. Tell others about Christ.
4. Worship, fellowship, and serve with other Christians in a church where Christ is preached.
5. As Christ's representative in a needy world, demonstrate your new life by your love and concern for others.

God bless you as you do.

Billy Graham

If you want further help in the decision you have made, write to:
Billy Graham Evangelistic Association
1 Billy Graham Parkway, Charlotte, North Carolina 28201-0001